A Christmas Wish

A collection of heart-warming short stories

By

Suzanne Rogerson

ISBN 9798364668509

TABLE OF CONTENTS

DEDICATION

I dedicate this book to my 'Santa Paws'.

Daisy has brought so much love into our lives and helped us through some difficult times. Every day she brings me joy. Thank you, Crazy Daisy, for inspiring me and for being you.

SANTA PAWS DELIVERY

'Dogs are not allowed in here.'

'Blaze isn't a normal dog.' Ella smiled pleasantly as she pointed to his harness, which stated in clear white letters, *Therapy Dog*.

'Some residents might be scared or allergic. This is a nursing home, not a pet shop,' the receptionist continued.

Ella looked down at Blaze and sucked in a calming breath.

He sat at her feet, patient and attentive, waiting on her command. She ruffled the black mop of hair on the spaniel's head, her composure restored. 'Blaze is a therapy dog. He comes in here every few weeks. The manager has already agreed to today's visit.'

The receptionist eyed Blaze warily, clearly not a dog lover. Blaze would normally win people over, but with the harness on, he was in work mode and on his best behaviour. He sat motionless, intelligent eyes focused only on Ella. Today, he wore a Santa Paws bandana over the white blaze on his chest.

Ella held up the red sack of presents. Each had been carefully chosen for individual residents on the "Victoria Wing" and wrapped with care for frail, arthritic hands to open. 'We're delivering these.'

The lady on the desk checked the papers in front of her. 'The Manager's off sick, so is the receptionist. I'm only a temp from the agency. No one left me any instructions about a dog visit.'

'The care workers on the "Victoria Wing" are aware of the arrangement. Why don't you speak to them?'

The receptionist still looked perplexed, but dutifully picked up the phone and dialled the extension number. Many rings later, she hung up and shrugged at Ella.

'The residents will be disappointed if we don't show up with their presents.'

'Fine, wait here. I'll go up and check.'

She used an ID card to let herself through the second set of security doors and glanced back hesitantly at them.

Ella offered the woman an encouraging smile.

When they were alone, Ella looked down at Blaze. 'Good boy.' He rested his head on her hand as she fussed over him.

He always sensed what she needed. She would never have got through the last two years without him. To think she'd never wanted a dog. Owning one had always been Rob's dream.

Her thoughts drifted back to those dark times when she hadn't wanted to get out of bed. Blaze was there, gently helping her through each day. Their walks around the park got her out into the world, and the brief hellos with fellow dog walkers gave her just enough human connection to survive the grief.

Ella pushed the thoughts aside and focused on the moment. Even in the reception area it was warm, and a hot flush crept across her skin. She fanned herself with her Christmas jumper, wishing she'd thought to wear the thin t-shirt style clothing rather than a thick knitted top.

The receptionist returned ten minutes later, breathing heavily. 'They're ready for you. If you could sign in the book, then you can go up.' She watched Blaze with a wary expression and her body language spoke of nervousness around dogs.

Ella softened towards the woman. 'Would you like to say hello? Blaze is very gentle. He's helped people work through phobias.'

'It's not a phobia... I just prefer cats.' The receptionist gave a nervous laugh and petted his head uncertainly. Blaze sat still, nudging his head ever so gently into her hand. The action drew a smile as the woman backed away. 'He's very cute,' she said as she settled behind the safety of her desk.

She buzzed Ella through the security door. 'Up the stairs, turn right...'

'It's okay, we know the way.'

Blaze knew where he was going and pulled on the lead until she gave a gentle command, reminding him to walk to heel.

They climbed the stairs rather than use the lift. After navigating the corridors of resident accommodation, they reached the community room at the end of the building. Background music played and a Christmas tree covered in tinsel stood in the corner.

Most of the residents were already gathered on the comfy chairs in the TV area. A few were even kitted out in Christmas jumpers. Ella paused in the doorway, waiting to ensure it was okay to come in.

Blaze's tail swished against her legs; even on his best behaviour, he could never completely control his excitement. When the residents saw him, they were the same. Grumpy, sad, quiet – none could resist the spaniel's charm.

Ella scanned the residents and spotted her gran sitting in her usual chair by the window. She appeared to be asleep, her wizened features relaxed and at peace.

The care worker, Crystal, looked up from clearing the table. She broke into a grin and nodded for Ella and Blaze to do the rounds.

Mrs Gaskin was the first to notice their arrival. Even though she was the care home's oldest resident, nothing escaped her gaze. She sat at the edge of the circle of chairs and waved them over.

Blaze stood against her leg and lifted his head so she could stroke him behind the ears. He was always gentle with her, as if mindful of her frail skin that bruised so easily. Her eyes lit up as she stroked him.

Next to her sat Humphrey. He bent down and gave Blaze a good scratch on the back. 'How's my boy doing?' Blaze licked Humphrey's face, making the old man laugh heartily.

Gwen was almost blind, but loved to play with the spaniel's silky, soft ears. He gave her his paw, which always made her smile, her milky eyes filling with tears.

They said a quick hello to the remaining residents in the "Victoria Wing" while Crystal finished helping everyone into the circle of comfortable armchairs. Ella and Blaze stood in the centre, red sack at the ready.

'Santa Paws and Ella have some very special deliveries today,' the care worker said loudly for those hard of hearing.

A few enthusiastic cheers followed, but her gran still hadn't stirred by the window. Crystal nodded. She would check on her and left Ella to begin.

'Blaze and I have been very busy selecting gifts for you all.'

She rummaged in the bag and pulled out the first present. 'This one is for Gwen.'

Blaze took the package gently in his mouth and she led him over to Gwen. Ella helped the blind woman take the gift and find a way to open it. A silky scarf fell onto her lap.

Gwen picked it up and held it against her cheek. 'It's as soft as Blaze's ears.' She put the scarf around her neck, beaming.

'It's a beautiful emerald green. The colour suits you,' Ella told her.

'Thank you, duck.' She shook Blaze's paw. 'You're such a clever boy.'

Next Humphrey opened a pair of novelty snowman bamboo socks, then Mrs Gaskin a jar of her favourite humbugs. She had no teeth and sucked them for hours while she watched old black and white films.

Blaze took the next parcel to Lizzy. Arthritis in her fingers made everyday tasks a struggle, but she didn't like to accept help, so Ella had used minimal tape to hold the paper together. Eventually, Lizzy unwrapped a festive box of diabetic shortbread.

Elsie opened her present next – a large print Agatha Christie book. 'Thank you, my dear. I haven't read one of these in years.'

'Next time I come, you'll have to tell me who did it.'

Elsie looked aghast as she hugged the novel to her chest. 'That's heresy. I could never spoil a book's ending.'

'Then I'd better borrow a copy from the library, and we can discuss it properly after I've read it.'

'That's a much better idea.'

Crystal came over to help the rest of the residents with their presents. She chatted in her jolly, outgoing way, which the residents couldn't help but respond to.

Ella pulled out another gift from the sack. 'Ah, this is a special gift for a very special person.' Blaze took the wrapped box in his mouth, and with Ella's direction, carried it to Crystal.

The nurse's cheeks bloomed with colour, and she got down on Blaze's level, making a big fuss of him. He licked her face and rewarded her with tail wags so strong his whole back end wiggled from side to side.

'These are my favourite. Thank you, Santa Paws,' Crystal said, holding onto her box of Milk Tray.

'I'll leave the other presents on the table,' Ella said, fishing out gifts for the other nurses.

Two presents remained in the sack. 'Mr Denan, Blaze has a gift for you too,' Ella said, waiting for the older man's reaction.

Mr Denan had been struggling to settle into the care home and didn't yet interact with the other residents. He hadn't paid much attention to Blaze on previous visits either, but he finally looked up now. Blaze wagged his tail in response to the acknowledgement. The old man nodded and held out his hand. With great care, Blaze took the parcel from Ella and dropped it into Mr Denan's waiting hands.

Blaze stayed close to the old man, knowing what was needed. Crazy, mad licks for Humphrey, gentle touches for Gwen, and now quiet comfort at Mr Denan's side.

Mr Denan opened the present, frowning. 'A chess set?'

It was a lightweight, magnetic chess set suitable for seniors. 'Your daughter said you used to play. It might give you something to do with the other residents. I know Humphrey enjoys a game, so does Elsie.'

They nodded.

'Nothing like a game of chess to test the little grey cells, Mr Denan,' Elsie said, patting her Poirot book.

Mr Denan sighed. 'If we're going to start playing together, you may as well call me Donald.'

They talked about chess while Crystal dragged over a small coffee table and set up the chess game with guidance from Donald. It was the most Ella had heard him talk, and she swallowed down emotion; she couldn't wait to report the progress back to his daughter.

Leaving them immersed in the game, she picked up the red sack and the remaining parcel left in the bottom.

She looked towards the window, hoping Crystal had managed to wake gran from her nap; she would hate to miss Blaze's visit.

Ella approached, catching sight of the view of the park. Winter bare trees hugged the edge of the open grassland. It was popular with dog walkers, though few had braved the cold today. A kiddies play area also looked forlorn and abandoned, while the winding stream cutting through the park looked majestic at any time of year. It was an inspiring sight even in the grip of a December chill, though it was also a reminder of the active lifestyle gran had been forced to leave behind after the stroke robbed her of full mobility.

Gran gazed out now, but Ella knew she was not really seeing – she was reliving her youth as head gardener at the park estate.

'Hi Gran.'

She turned towards Ella, her eyes blank of recognition. Blaze sat against gran's leg, gentle and quiet, waiting for her to respond.

A hand reached down to pat his head, and he licked her fingers. A small smile curled her lips.

'Ella,' she whispered.

'Happy Christmas, Gran. I've brought Blaze to see everyone today. He has some special deliveries.'

Gran ran her bony fingers through the long, glossy fur on the spaniel's head and admired his festive bandana.

'How's my little granddaughter?'

Ella laughed. 'Not so little. I turned forty-four this year – remember I told you.'

'Time doesn't mean much in here, dear.'

Ella didn't rise to the bait; gran and her morbid thoughts were legendary in the "Victoria Wing".

'What are you doing with yourself nowadays?'

'Blaze's therapy work is keeping me busy. And visiting you, of course.'

'Are we going for a walk today?'

'Not today. It's a little chilly. I know you don't like the cold.'

The older woman shivered involuntarily. 'I hate the cold, and I hate these gloomy winter days when nothing grows.'

'It'll be spring before we know it.'

Gran shrugged her bony shoulders. 'Seasons aren't what they were in my day. We always had a white Christmas when I was a girl. I loved the snow before I got old and useless.'

'There's talk of a white Christmas in the news.'

'News! They don't know their arse from their elbow, those lot.' She waved dismissively at the television.

Blaze's tail thumped against their legs, picking up on gran's sour mood. The old lady stroked him with her good hand, the motion bringing calm to her expression.

'Blaze has a busy week. Tomorrow we're going to the children's hospice and on Christmas Eve we're going to visit the children's ward to deliver presents to them.'

'He's a good boy, just like my Bonzo.' She sounded wistful as she ruffled the spaniel's fur. 'Expect I'll be seeing him soon.'

Ella squeezed gran's hand. She'd been saying as much for years, but one day they both knew it would come true. Death was closer than most people wanted to admit. Sometimes it struck out of the blue and snuffed out a vibrant life much too soon.

She looked at all the residents, knowing most of them were widowed too; she never thought it would happen to her so young.

Ella forced down her emotions. 'Blaze has a present for you.'

Gran took the gift from Blaze and tore it open. It was a shawl made from the softest wool dyed a dusky pink.

'Thank you, sweetheart. It's very nice.'

She helped gran try it on before folding the shawl on the arm of the chair. 'You can wear it next time I visit. We'll go to the park and feed the ducks.'

Gran smiled at that and lay her head back against the chair as she stared out of the window. 'That'll be nice, dear. I still like the ducks, can't see them from up here though.'

The lunch trolley was wheeled in, signalling Ella's time to leave.

'Your Christmas lunch is here, Gran, and it smells delicious. Let's get you to the table.'

The other residents were chatting happily as they were helped into their seats.

Gran sat between Elsie and Donald, who were still talking about chess.

Crackers and paper hats were being distributed by the staff who helped the residents pull them and read out the silly jokes.

Blaze said goodbye to each of them.

Ella kissed her gran on the cheek and left, pausing in the doorway to look back at the festive scene. Even Donald looked like he was starting to enjoy himself.

'They are always so much happier after your visits,' Crystal said as they shared a goodbye hug outside the social room.

'It's not me, it's all down to Blaze.'

'I don't know. I think you've trained him to care and we're very grateful.'

Ella smiled down at Blaze. 'He's the best. One in a million.'

'So are you, Ella. Take care.'

Crystal knew about her husband's death and how Ella coped with her grief by looking after others. It was better that way – to focus on what she could do rather than what was out of her control. She squeezed their two wedding bands kept on a chain around her neck, certain Rob would be proud of her.

She returned to the reception desk and signed out.

The temp smiled more openly as she handed over a card and two wrapped presents – one suspiciously bone-shaped.

'Sorry about earlier. No one told me to expect you. This is from everyone here, by the way. Happy Christmas.'

'Ah, thank you.' Ella took the presents and placed them in the sack, touched by the gesture.

Outside the nursing home, the grey sky looked laden with snow clouds. The prediction of a white Christmas seemed more likely by the minute.

She ruffled Blaze's fur. 'You did good today.'

His tongue lolled out, and he panted happily as he gazed up at her. Sometimes she thought she saw Rob's spirit staring out from Blaze's soulful, knowing brown eyes.

She smiled sadly. The familiar weight of grief she carried in her chest was still there, but she was getting used to the burden.

'Come on, boy, let's go home.'

They cut through the park where she let Blaze off the lead.

In full dog mode, he ran through the grass with his nose down, before heading to his favourite spot amongst the trees to chase squirrels.

She watched his antics, grinning to herself. To some, he may just be a dog, but to Ella he was everything. He'd touched people's lives and brought joy to lonely hearts. He was a real-life Santa Paws.

Christmas Wish - Part One

'Attention everyone.'

Cassie watched as her boss, red-faced and tipsy, pranced across the makeshift karaoke stage at the back of the pub. He tapped the microphone, which crackled and screeched.

'Sorry.' He shouted just as someone turned down the Christmas music.

'Grab your drinks and gather round.'

Cassie took her wine from the bar and stood at the back. Lynn, her best friend, sidled up beside her, pulling a face. 'This'll be good.'

Cassie hid a snigger as Derek launched into his speech. Polite laughter followed his lame attempts at humour. Not that Derek was a bad boss, he just wasn't very inventive - same venue, same food, same speech every year.

She hid a yawn behind her hand.

Lynn nudged her. 'You're slow tonight.' By the slur in Lynn's voice, Cassie knew she'd already consumed enough alcohol for them both.

'I'm not feeling it.' She stifled another yawn; she needed the two-week Christmas break. Lie in's, no commute - bliss.

'Where's Cassie?' Derek's words filtered into her thoughts.

Lynn waved helpfully. Cassie wanted to melt into the floorboards along with the sticky stains beneath her feet.

'Cassie's been working on a special project for me. Thanks to her, tonight is an extra celebration. With this new contract secured, I'm pleased to announce this year's Christmas bonus is doubled!'

Enthusiastic cheers rang out and glasses were raised in her direction.

'When I step down next year, I know the company will be in good hands.'

Cassie forced a smile, her cheeks blazing. Ten years she'd coveted that role, but now she only had one dream, and it wasn't being CEO of Derek's company.

'The next round's on me.' Derek's words sparked a mad scramble for the bar.

Disco lights flashed, and the music throbbed. The smell of party nibbles and spilt beer mingled, and she fought back nausea. 'I need some air.'

Lynn took her arm and barged through the throng of people to the door. Outside, cool, fresh air washed over them.

'Better?'

She nodded.

Her friend sipped her drink, rubbing a bare arm as the winter chill wrapped around them. 'I'm booking myself a winter sun getaway with that bonus. What about you?'

'IVF. We're going to try again in the new year.'

'Oh, Cass.' Lynn squeezed her hand. 'It'll happen one day.'

She tried to smile, but there was an empty ache inside her only a baby could fix. 'Two years we've tried. It's like we're not meant to be parents.'

'Rubbish, you and Scott will be great parents.'

'I hope so, otherwise it'll be me up there making awful speeches every Christmas.' When did she lose her passion for the job? Around the time her biological clock kicked in, she supposed.

Cassie sipped warm wine. Grimacing, she tossed it away.

'Are you sure you're okay? You've been looking peaky recently.'

'Just overworked. I can't wait to spend the day in bed.'

Lynn downed her drink. 'Best have something to recover from then.' She cackled, her laugh always turned filthy after a few rums.

'Actually, I'm heading home.'

'You can't leave me. I wanted your help to put the moves on Hot Harry.'

'You don't need my help. And I'm tired. I might be coming down with something.'

Lynn squinted at her. 'Are you sure you're not pregnant already?'

'It's hardly likely. I've been working too hard to bother trying.'

'My sister acted like this when she fell. When was your last period?'

'I don't know… a while ago. They're so irregular I lose track.'

'Maybe it's a Christmas wish come true.'

'Don't.' She didn't want to get her hopes up, but anticipation fizzed in her belly all the same.

Lynn disappeared inside and returned with their coats and handbags. 'There's a late-night chemist up the road.'

'I can't do it now.'

'Course you can.'

Ten minutes later, Cassie found herself back in the pub, perched over the toilet, peeing on a stick.

'Hurry up, I'm busting,' Lynn called through the door.

Cassie left the stall, the pregnancy test hidden in her bag. Suddenly overwhelmed, she couldn't bear to find out while surrounded by drunken colleagues. 'I'm going home.'

'Wait, I can't stop mid-flow.'

'Sorry. Call you tomorrow.'

Cassie snuck out the back of the pub. She squeezed the strap of her handbag as she ran to the tube station, too scared to look at the result. Every negative took her closer to the CEO role and further from her dream of motherhood.

She needed to get home. Scott knew how to make the darkness go away.

***

'Hi.'

Scott looked up from watching TV. 'That finished early. How was it?'

'When you've been to one piss up...' She shrugged. 'Fancy putting the kettle on while I get changed?'

'Sure.'

Upstairs, she stripped off the party dress that emphasised her flat, empty stomach and tossed it on

~ 16 ~

the bed. Pulling on her favourite flannelette PJ's, she felt a little better, though her hand still shook as she reached for her handbag.

Two cooling cups of tea waited on the coffee table when she eventually returned. Scott lifted the throw, and they snuggled together on the sofa.

She handed him a small parcel.

'What's this?'

'A gift.'

'It's not Christmas yet.'

'So?'

Scott grinned and tore at the Christmas wrapping paper like a little boy. Two plastic sticks fell onto his lap. Turning them over, he stared at two sets of identical blue lines.

'Does this mean…'

'We're pregnant!'

He squeezed her in a hug. 'My god, how?'

She laughed. 'You've had enough practice to work that out for yourself.'

'I can't believe it.'

'Our wish finally came true.' The words caught in her throat. This time next year they'd be a family; the promotion would have to wait.

'This is the best gift I could ever ask for.' Scott nuzzled her neck. 'I'll miss all that practice, though.'

Cassie kissed him, all trace of tiredness gone. 'I'm still up for a little practice if you are.'

FOR THE HOLIDAYS

'Molly, stop wriggling.'

'But it hurts.'

'It's only a splinter.'

'Ow, stop it.'

'I'm only trying to help you.'

'I don't need your help.' Molly wrenched her hand away.

Frankie swallowed down the hurt. 'At least let me put some cream on it in case it gets infected.'

'I don't care if it does.'

'Molly…'

'Leave me alone, you're not my mother.' She stormed away, slamming the kitchen door behind her for effect.

Frankie sighed as she packed away the first aid kit and stored it back in the cupboard. As she prepared dinner, she glanced out of the window and saw Molly sitting on the swing seat again, despite getting a splinter from it in the first place. Tim really should dismantle the rickety old thing they'd inherited with the house. Molly could help them choose a new one in the spring when they renovated the garden.

It was cold and Molly wasn't wearing a coat. Frankie bit down on the urge to interfere. The last thing she wanted was to be seen as a nag - it was hard enough finding equilibrium in their new relationship.

What kind of Christmas were they going to have if her stepdaughter didn't even want to be in the same room as her?

She tried not to think about tomorrow. Instead, she reached for a packet of cookies like her own mum used to do, but hesitated. Did Molly even like milk and cookies? She had no clue what the brooding thirteen-year-old liked.

Frankie glanced at the phone and considered calling Tim. He'd said he would be in a business meeting all day, trying to wrap up the sale so he could take the Christmas holidays off. She couldn't run to him every time she had a problem with his daughter. Maybe Molly just needed space to cool off. They had all been thrust into this strange situation and had to find a way to get along.

Once the stew was in the oven, Frankie poured a glass of ice-cold milk and put three chocolate chip cookies on a plate. She found Molly lying on the sofa flicking through music channels on the TV.

'How's the finger?'

'Fine.' Molly settled on a channel playing grunge. She looked up through a mop of blonde hair as if waiting for a complaint.

Frankie smiled, remembering when she was the same age rebelling against her parents. 'I loved Nirvana growing up.'

Molly tried not to look impressed. 'They're okay, I s'pose.'

'I thought you might like a snack.'

'Mum doesn't like me snacking before dinner.'

'Let's make it a one off then. We don't want to waste these yummy cookies.'

Molly took the offering with a muttered thank you and Frankie left her to it, not wanting to push her luck.

She hummed 'Come As You Are' as she finished the preparation for dinner, hoping somehow music could help her bond with her stepdaughter. She thought back to her own childhood; Mum had made it all look so easy. She'd left a difficult legacy for Frankie to live up to. She pushed down the pang of loss and focused on their revised plans for Christmas now that Molly was joining them for the duration of the holidays.

Molly came out to the kitchen, rinsed the glass and plate and left them by the sink. She huffed and paced the length of the room, opening cupboards and sighing heavily. 'It's so boring here. When's dad back from work?'

'He should be back by five. Shall we find something to do until then?'

Molly shrugged.

Frankie wandered into the front room and looked around. It was all very adult and orderly, no sign that it was meant to be a family home. Apart from the tree lights flashing in the corner, there wasn't much sign of Christmas either.

She put herself in Molly's shoes, dumped in a place she didn't know and expected to fit in. 'How about we redecorate the tree and surprise your dad?'

'Why? It looks fine.'

'Yes, but it's a bit plain, don't you think? I'm sure we can jazz it up.'

Molly shrugged again. 'Whatever. I've got nothing better to do.'

Frankie went to the storage room and rummaged around until she found the shoebox she'd seen when they got out the Christmas lights. She hoped Molly would appreciate the gesture and not throw it back in her face.

Molly took the box, her mouth opening silently as she realised what it was. She pulled out an old cardboard bauble covered in painted pasta shells, a glittery snowflake, and a wooden Christmas tree painted green with white dots for snow and wiggly red lines for tinsel. There were lots of other homemade decorations and an angel.

'This is all the old stuff I made for dad. I thought he'd chucked them.'

'He would never do that. Let's find space for them on the tree.'

They worked in companionable silence, positioning each piece with care amongst the red and gold baubles.

'We'll have to throw this away.' Molly held out the angel. Both her wings were broken.

'She looks a bit sad for herself, but we can fix that.'

Frankie grabbed her supplies, and they'd soon fixed the wings with tape and cardboard support. She gave the angel pride of place on top of the tree and then stood back to examine it. 'Now it's perfect.'

Molly nodded. 'I remember dad's old Christmas tree at the flat. It was a bit pathetic. This one's much nicer.'

Frankie remembered the spindly tree she'd made Tim throw out. Their new house deserved a proper six-foot, snow-dusted Christmas tree.

'Here's some tinsel. Let's drape it over everything and make the place more festive.'

Pictures, mirrors, lamps, coffee table and fireplace, even the tv was given a sparkly facelift.

She shot a sideways glance at Molly as they finished; they'd gone a full half an hour without complaints of boredom. 'How are your baking skills?'

'I don't have any.'

'Well, how about we make a batch of mince pies? I always used to make them with my mum on Christmas Eve.' She smiled to herself at the treasured memory.

'Mum never bothers making anything like that. She says they're cheap enough to buy, anyway.'

'It's fun to make them though, and they taste much better homemade. I could teach you if you like.'

Molly looked a little nervous. 'Okay.'

'Wash your hands and put this on while I get all the ingredients together.'

Minutes later, Molly was ready in an apron with her hair tied back. 'What now?'

'We need some ambience.' Frankie put on a radio channel playing Christmas hits.

Molly rolled her eyes.

'Only joking.' They opted for a rock channel and hummed along as they measured and mixed the pastry into a ball. Once the dough had rested in the fridge for ten minutes, she let Molly do the rolling and cutting. They stuffed each little pastry case with a spoon of mincemeat from a jar.

'I used to think they were disgusting. I thought they were made of real meat,' Molly admitted, her cheeks flushing.

'Oh, everyone makes that mistake.' Frankie smiled. 'My mum used to make her own special mincemeat. I never did get the recipe.'

She showed Molly how to fit the tops and brush them with milk.

Molly looked proud as she finished the rest and they put the two trays in the oven. 'I'm going to make these for Mum next year... if she's home for Christmas.'

The mood sobered, and Frankie silently cursed Tim's ex. So what if she could get a great deal on a last-minute holiday? She should have taken Molly with her.

'I'm sure your mum won't make a habit of going away every Christmas.'

Molly pouted as she dragged her finger through the flour on the side, making figures of eight shapes.

'Here, you have flour on your face.' Frankie reached over and splatted a dollop of flour on Molly's nose.

Molly giggled as she wiped it away. 'You're mad.'

'I try my best.'

'How long do the mince pies cook for?'

'I bake them for about twenty minutes, but I always set a timer early so I don't forget.'

'I'm going to my room for a bit then.'

'Oh, okay.' Frankie nodded, caught off guard. 'I'll give you a shout when they're done.'

Molly ran up the stairs without another word and the door shut resoundingly behind her.

Frankie washed up, not sure what had just happened. She'd thought they'd made a connection.

She pottered around the kitchen, waiting on the timer. 'Pies are done,' she called from the bottom of the stairs.

'I'll have one later,' Molly called back.

At least she wasn't being given the silent treatment. She'd heard horror stories from other stepparents who went days without speaking to their stepfamily. She rolled the wedding ring around her finger and looked at the picture of the three of them on the day. Molly had been easy-going about their wedding that summer and seemed to enjoy being a bridesmaid. But Frankie still felt a distance between them; sometimes she wondered if she would ever find a way to breech it.

She was just dusting the cooled mince pies with icing sugar when Tim arrived home.

'That's me done until the New Year. How have things been here?'

'Fine, or so I thought. I don't understand. We were making progress, but now she's staying in her room.'

'It'll take time. She hasn't been great with change since the divorce.'

'I suppose.' Frankie nodded.

'This is a triple whammy - new step mum, new house, a whole new Christmas routine to get used to.'

'I know, it's just I really wanted to make our first Christmas as a family special.'

'You're doing great.' He kissed her and hugged her close. 'She's still a little miffed at why her mum suddenly decided not to spend Christmas with her. Swanning off to France like that at such short notice was very unfair of Anne.'

Frankie didn't understand it either. She would never have abandoned her child to go on holiday over the festive period. It secretly reinforced her suspicions that Anne was a very selfish parent.

'Why don't I go see how she's doing?' Tim offered.

'Take a couple of these with you. They're still warm.' She handed him a plate with two of the mince pies they'd baked earlier.

'They smell delicious.'

'Molly did most of the work. I hope she likes them.' The pies were all evenly shaped, and the filling had only seeped through the gaps in the pastry on a couple of them - not bad for a first attempt. 'Don't force her to come down if she doesn't want to. I want her to enjoy herself here.'

'She'll come around.' He gave her a quick hug. 'You worry too much, darling.'

Easy for Tim to say; he didn't have to contend with the constant fear of spoiling the close relationship between father and daughter.

While he went upstairs to check on Molly, she poured a small glass of wine and set the table for dinner.

Tim returned and nicked a sip of her drink.

She smacked his bum. 'Get your own.'

Tim grabbed a fresh glass and topped them both up. 'Molly will be down in five minutes. She asked if we could continue an old family tradition of opening a present on Christmas Eve.'

'That sounds lovely.'

They took their drinks into the front room to wait. The soft lighting allowed the tree to take centre stage, while its flashing lights picked out the tinsel they'd liberally doused around the room.

'Someone's been busy.' Tim admired the tree, picking up one of the old decorations Molly had made. A wistful look flickered across his face. 'Thank you for doing this.'

Frankie moved next to him and squeezed his hand. 'We're a family. I want Molly to be part of it.'

She sat in one of the new armchairs while Tim lit the fire. Instantly, the room felt cosy. It was the perfect home, and she realised it felt more complete with Molly there too.

If she could have one Christmas wish, it would be for their small family to get along over the holidays.

Molly arrived and offered a shy smile as she sat on the sofa opposite. She tucked her hair behind her ear and clutched two presents on her lap.

Tim bent down by the tree and pulled out a present for his daughter.

Molly opened it and grinned as she held the fluffy dressing gown to her face. 'It's perfect.'

Tim opened his next, a musical Christmas jumper, which he pledged to wear over Christmas lunch.

Her stepdaughter handed Frankie the second gift.

'Oh, thank you.' She hadn't been expecting anything and swallowed back the lump in her throat.

'Open it.' Molly looked on nervously as Frankie carefully ripped open the package.

It was a painting on a small square of canvas. Delicate brush strokes depicted a peaceful Christmas scene. On the edge of the canvas was a decorated tree, and in the centre, a coffee table with a plate of mince pies sat in front of a fireplace. The orange glow of the fire gave the picture a warm feeling. The skill of the thirteen-year-old astounded her. It was a world away from the pasta painted baubles they'd hung on the tree earlier.

'Sorry, it was rushed,' Molly said with a dismissive flick of her wrist.

Seeing the paint stains under Molly's fingernails, Frankie realised that was why she'd locked herself away in her room; it wasn't that she wanted to be somewhere else at all. Tears pricked Frankie's eyes.

'It's beautiful, I love it. It will always remind me of our first Christmas together.'

Molly looked at her lap, tucking stray hairs behind her ears.

Frankie's heart melted. She gave the painting pride of place on the mantelpiece while she gathered her emotions.

'For a step mum, you're pretty cool.'

'Thank you.' Frankie smiled at her stepdaughter and sat back in the armchair, certain she was glowing as brightly as the Christmas lights.

Tim put his arm around Molly's shoulders. 'What about me? I'm hip too, aren't I?'

Molly looked at Frankie and they both burst out laughing.

'Don't push it, Dad.'

'Hey.' He swooped on Molly and tickled her mercilessly.

Frankie grinned, watching Tim and his daughter. From the corner of her eye, she glimpsed the painting on the mantlepiece.

It looked like they would make it through Christmas just fine.

CHANCE ENCOUNTERS

'I don't ask much of you. You barely go to school. What kind of job are you going to get? You don't wanna be a layabout like your dad. The only thing he's good at is getting in trouble with the law.'

'Give it a rest, mum. I'll pass those stupid exams if it makes you happy.'

'I want you to get into college and make something of yourself.' Mum rushed out of the kitchen, buttoning up her coat as she went. 'Where did I put that damn ID badge?'

'She just wants us both to do well,' Alfie said, seeing the angry scowl on Lee's face.

'Shut up. I don't need you butting in.'

Lee put his bowl of soup in the sink and followed mum from the room. 'I'm busy tonight, can't Alfie stay by himself?'

'No Lee, he's ten-years-old. I need these extra shifts before Christmas. The least you can do is mind your brother while I earn enough to feed you both.'

Alfie got between them. 'I'll be old enough to have a paper round soon, then you won't have to work so much.'

'You're a sweet boy.' Mum kissed him on the head. She looked tired; she always did. 'Be good for your brother. I won't be back until late.'

Lee pulled a face at him. Mum saw and grabbed Lee in a hug before ruffling his hair. 'Thanks babe.'

'Whatever.' Lee disappeared into their bedroom with his phone.

Alfie washed the soup bowls - mum always hated it when they were left to go hard and crusty. He sat down in front of the TV, flicking through channels until he found a Christmas episode of The Simpsons.

Lee stood in front of him and tossed him a Santa hat and a red scarf.

'What's this for?'

'We're going out. Come on.'

'But it's dark.'

'It's not even six o'clock, don't be such a baby.'

'But…'

'Look, we're going out to earn some money… buy mum a Christmas present.'

'How?'

'Doesn't matter. Hurry up, my mates are waiting.'

'Who…'

'You don't know them. Just hurry up.'

They locked up the flat and Alfie rushed down the stairs after Lee, lagging behind his brother's lanky stride.

Three boys were waiting outside the block. They looked much older, so Alfie stuck close to Lee.

'What's this bruv?' The one who appeared to be the leader sneered at Alfie. 'This ain't no babysitting gig.'

Alfie stayed put, but he didn't look at anyone directly.

'This is Alfie, my brother.'

'I can see that. Why'd yer bring him?'

'He's gonna sing for us. Don't worry, he's decent, Jonny.'

Alfie stood a little taller at the hint of pride in his brother's voice.

'Hope he sings better than he talks.' One of the others laughed and nudged Jonny.

'I guarantee he's better than you lot.' Lee punched Alfie on the arm. It wasn't hard, just for show, so Alfie didn't mind.

'Go on then.' Jonny shoved the collection bucket at him. 'Prove you can sing at the first house. If you're rubbish, you can both get lost.'

Lee shrugged, and they started walking. The others chatted, but Alfie didn't pay much attention as he nervously clutched the bucket handle.

'I've never been carol singing before,' he whispered to Lee.

His brother rolled his eyes. 'Just sing. No one cares. They pay to get rid of you.'

They walked a few blocks away from the flats to a residential road filled with houses that had Christmas lights flashing in every window.

Jonny knocked at the first house. When the door opened, he nudged Alfie to get singing.

A young couple and their baby stared at him while a bulldog nosed at him from between their legs.

Alfie took a deep breath. 'We wish you a merry Christmas...' he began tentatively.

The rest of the gang joined in, out of sync and out of tune. Alfie remembered singing at Christmas assemblies at school. It was so much easier with the teachers counting time and the rest of the class masking any little mistakes.

As they finished their awful rendition, he held out the bucket and smiled like his brother had instructed. Coins jangled with others in the bottom – Jonny had explained they were planted to make it look like the neighbours were giving generously.

Alfie could see Lee was right. They were being paid to go away; the singing was terrible.

He thanked the couple, and the group walked away. He heard the others muttering behind him.

'Not worth it. Family, dogs…'

'Nice cars in the drive, though.'

'No, avoid the ones with dogs.'

They walked to the next house, sang not quite so terribly, and collected a few pounds for their trouble.

'What are they talking about?' Alfie asked his brother when the others continued to discuss the houses.

'Don't worry about it. It's just messing around.'

They walked up the path to the next house. Christmas lights were flashing in the window, and he could see a big tree in the front room almost touching the ceiling.

A man answered and stood with crossed arms as they sang "We Three Kings".

They collected more small change and tried the next few houses with similar results.

'Do all these places have stupid cameras?' one of them muttered.

'Half of them probably aren't even plugged in. Don't stress, Ben,' Jonny said as he led them out of the cul-de-sac.

They hadn't even gone to every house, and Alfie asked why.

'You can just tell when they aren't gonna pay,' Jonny said over his shoulder.

'Idiot,' Ben muttered.

'Yeah, your job is to sing, not ask stupid questions.'

Lee nudged his arm. 'Don't worry about them. None of them can sing like you.'

The second and third roads were just as productive, especially when Jonny told them it was for charity.

It didn't seem right to lie, but they had no money, so it was like charity in a way. He wanted to get mum a nice Christmas present. She worked so hard to pay the bills and he wanted to make her happy this Christmas.

Several houses said no thanks and shut the door before they could even lie about the charity. Others asked for more songs as if to test them, but Alfie knew most carols. He often sang with mum when she was cooking their dinner - she said it helped her relax after work.

A few roads later, they stopped under a streetlight to check the haul. 'About thirty-five quid,' Jonny said.

'Don't forget the mince pies,' Alfie reminded them. A smiling old couple had offered them mince pies, which only Alfie and Lee had taken, scoffing them as they walked.

'This is crap. I could be inside on my Xbox.'

'This next road should be better, Marv. Bungalows mean old people. They like a bit of singing,' Jonny said with a grin.

'Easy targets,' Marv agreed. 'They're probably deaf as well.'

'Good job,' Lee said, looking over at Alfie. 'You sounded like a strangled cat singing Silent Night, Ben.'

Ben flashed him a warning look. 'Don't push it, mate.'

Jonny slung his arm around Lee's shoulders. 'The trouble is, he ain't wrong. Luckily, we have Alfie along.'

They swaggered down the road, teasing each other. Alfie enjoyed being singled out by their leader, but he still didn't get why they were so bothered checking out the homes. Just because someone had nice things didn't mean they would tip well.

At the top of the road, they pulled their Santa hats low and scarfs high. It wasn't even that cold, considering it was almost Christmas.

'Go on then, Alf. Do your stuff.' Jonny pushed him forward.

Several houses later, there was more change in the bucket. 'Can we stop now?' Alfie wanted to get home before mum did.

'There's plenty more bungalows to try before we quit, choir boy.' Jonny teased him and Alfie didn't complain again, not wanting to look childish.

A few of the old people were nervous and didn't open their doors past the security chain. Others didn't come to the door at all, even though they could hear the tv's playing and see the lights were on.

One old man watched them sing, holding onto his walking stick and the doorframe for support. He didn't look well, but he smiled along as Alfie led the singing.

'Thank you for the song.' The old man fumbled in his pocket for change and dropped it all over the floor.

Alfie helped him pick it up. The man's hands were cold as he took the money and put it in the collection bucket.

'Are you okay?' Alfie asked quietly, hoping the others wouldn't hear and tease him for caring.

'I'm fine lad.' His hands were shaky as he shut the door.

They finished the road, having only been able to sing at another two houses. The rest refused to answer.

'It's getting late. People will be getting too wary to answer their doors now,' Lee said. 'And I should get my brother home.'

Jonny gave him a look. 'That wasn't the plan.'

The older kids started talking in hushed voices while Lee pulled him aside. 'Here's a tenner's worth of change. Why don't you stop at the shop on the way home? Buy those chocolates for mum and hide them under the bed.'

'Why can't I stay with you?'

'We're gonna buy booze and drink it over the park. You're too young.'

'So are you.'

'Go home. I don't want you in trouble.'

The angry glint warned Alfie not to argue any further. He pocketed the money and headed away.

'Cheers Alfie,' Jonny called after him.

The others were laughing and pushing each other as they walked off.

He heard them mention easy targets again and turned back to see them heading for the alleyway behind the bungalows. There were no shops that way and it was in the opposite direction to the park.

Alfie followed them into the mouth of the alley, swallowing down fear. He could hear them whispering as they counted the gates and got a bad feeling in his stomach.

It was really dark with only the stars to see by, and he instantly regretted coming after them.

'What are you doing?' he asked as he caught up to them. They'd stopped outside a gate. Someone was wrestling with the latch.

'Piss off, kid,' he recognised Ben's deep tone and felt the threat in the words.

'No, this isn't right. Why are you doing this, Lee?'

'Shut up. No names,' Lee hissed at him.

'You can't do this.'

'Shut your brother up, mate, or we will,' Jonny said, his voice cold and hard.

Lee pulled him aside. 'This is their idea, to get some easy money.'

'But it's wrong. You'll end up inside, like dad.'

'You heard mum. What use am I? School doesn't care about kids like me. I'll never get a decent job...'

'It doesn't mean you have to rob people.'

Lee huffed in the darkness.

'I'm not leaving you.' Alfie crossed his arms; he couldn't walk away even though he was really scared of what the others would do to him.

Jonny and his minions had rammed the gate and let themselves into the garden.

He grabbed Lee's arm. 'You have to stop them.'

He could sense his brother's hesitation. Lee had never wanted to break the law before. They'd both seen what it did to mum when their dad was put inside.

'They won't listen to me.'

'You can still try.'

He felt Lee nod and released his grip. They followed the others through the gate. It was pitch black. The garden had no security lights, just a bare bulb shining through the kitchen window. Sneaking down the path, Alfie's stomach knotted in fear.

What if a neighbour looked out and saw them? What if the police came and arrested them all? The urge to run was strong, but he gritted his teeth. Lee had taught him to stand up to the bullies at school who said cruel things about their family. He could stand up to these bigger boys, too.

The others had already reached the backdoor. Someone was using the muted light of their phone to check out the door. It had an old wooden frame with a glass panel that looked easy to smash. Someone tried the handle first, it wasn't locked.

'Wait,' Lee whispered, but they crept inside without listening.

The telly was blaring out and there were lights on in the hall and front room.

'Shit!' Ben whispered.

The four of them had come to a stop. Alfie had to force his way between them.

He saw a pair of slippered feet in the hall. An old man was lying flat out, not moving.

'Oh my god, he's dead, man!' Marv pushed past them and raced out of the back door. The other two followed but Alfie's legs weren't working.

Lee grabbed his arm and tried to tug him away.

'But shouldn't we see if he's okay?'

Lee cursed. He dropped to his knees by the body and felt the old man's neck.

'Well?' Alfie whispered, too scared to raise his voice.

Lee sat back and ran a hand through his hair. 'There's a pulse.' He stood and paced around the prone old man.

'Should we call someone?'

'We need to get him into the recovery position first.'

Alfie nodded, waiting for his big brother's lead.

'Help me put him on his side, and then we make sure he's breathing.' They worked together; it was surprising how heavy the old man was.

'Get the phone and call 999. We can run once the ambulance is coming.'

Alfie froze. 'We can't leave him like this.'

'We have no business being here, we'll be arrested.' Lee grabbed the phone himself from the table in the hall. 'You wanna go to juvie?'

Alfie shook his head.

Lee dialled and then turned away to focus on the call. 'I need an ambulance.'

While his brother talked, Alfie sat silently by the old man, watching his chest rise and fall. He had a bump on the head, but he couldn't see what else was wrong with him. His skin was pale, even his lips.

'I think he's cold,' Alfie said aloud. He took off his coat and lay it across the old man, even though it didn't quite cover him.

Lee was still explaining the situation on the phone. 'Yes, it's Manor Gardens, house number…' he had to open the front door to check '…twenty-three. I don't know the old guy's name… we're just… carol singers…'

Lee frowned across at Alfie and then walked into the front room. Alfie hoped he wasn't still considering robbing the old man.

The others would have done.

He swallowed. What if Jonny and the others came back? The back door was still open. He could feel the chilly air seeping inside the building.

He raced through to the kitchen and looked around before slamming the door shut, twisting the lock and testing the handle from the inside.

Heart pounding, he returned to see his brother bent down over the old man. He was tucking a tartan blanket around him. He looked up and threw Alfie his coat. 'The ambulance is coming,' he said, holding his hand over the phone and indicating to the door with his head.

'No, we're not family.' He continued answering questions. 'I told you I don't know the guy, or what happened to him. He's on the floor out cold, looks real bad.'

Alfie could hear the operator talking calmly, asking if the patient had any medical bracelets or a necklace.

Lee clenched his jaw. 'Hold on.'

Alfie helped him check the old man's wrists and neck.

'Nothing,' he reported back. 'Yes, he's still breathing. He looks like he's sleeping. I don't know… he just collapsed.' He looked at Alfie and shrugged helplessly. 'How long is the ambulance going to take? Twenty minutes. Can't they get here sooner?'

Alfie leant closer and could hear the operator talking. 'Just make him as comfortable as you can. We can stay on the line while you wait.'

Lee stood and paced; his jaw set in an angry line. Then he crossed to the table by the phone and grabbed the post sitting there. 'I know his name. It's Mr Cyril Wilson.'

'Have you tried to rouse him?' The operator asked.

'No.'

'Call his name, speaking loudly but calmly.'

Alfie leant over him. 'Mr Wilson, can you hear me?' He asked several times without getting a response.

Lee gave him a gentle shake. 'Mr Wilson... yes, his eyes just flickered. I think he's coming round.' Lee was instantly calmer. 'Mr Wilson, everything is okay. An ambulance is on its way to help you.'

The old man groaned. His eyes struggled to open, and then he fixed his gaze on Alfie. 'What? What happened?'

'You had a fall, Mr Wilson,' Alfie said.

'I'm cold.' He looked frightened and tried to move.

Lee got a cushion from the front room and gently put it under his head. 'I think you should stay there, wait for help. Okay?'

Mr Wilson nodded.

Alfie held his hand; it always made him feel better when he was scared.

'What should we do now?' Lee asked the operator.

'You're doing great. Just keep him talking. The ambulance will be with you very soon.'

Within minutes, Lee was letting in the paramedics. The lady paramedic started assessing Mr Wilson by asking him lots of questions, while the male paramedic took the old man's pulse and checked him over.

Alfie could feel his brother itching to run out of the open door to get away before any police were involved with awkward questions. But Alfie wanted to make sure old Mr Wilson would be okay before they left.

Lee watched the paramedics work without speaking.

'Are you on any medication, Mr Wilson?'

He shook his head.

'Does anyone else live with you?'

He shook his head again.

'Do you have any pain…'

Eventually, satisfied he hadn't broken anything in the fall, they carefully eased the old man onto a stretcher and strapped him in with a blanket to keep warm. The lady paramedic was still talking to Mr Wilson, but the other paramedic turned to them. He was big and intimidating, but he had a kind face and smiling eyes.

'You lads have been very brave tonight. Well done. You did all the right things.'

'I did first aid at school last term,' Lee said.

'You're clearly a paramedic in the making. Are you family?'

'No, we're just carol singers,' Lee said quickly.

The lady looked up as they were talking before turning back to her patient. 'Can we inform your next of kin, Mr Wilson? Let them know where we're taking you?'

He looked confused. 'I don't know the number.'

Alfie's gaze fell on an address book sat on the little table next to the telephone. He tried to give it to the old man, but his hand snaked out of the blanket and grabbed Alfie's arm instead.

The confusion lifted from his expression. 'Lovely voice, this one. Sung my wife's favourite carol. She used to sing in the church choir, you know.' He told the paramedic, his eyes watering. 'I miss all those carols and midnight mass...' He kept hold of Alfie's arm as he talked; Alfie didn't mind.

The lady smiled at him. 'Do you have family, Mr Wilson? Someone we can call?'

'My daughter, Helen Wilson. In the book.'

The male paramedic took the address book and called the daughter to explain. '...Two young lads are with him. They've done a fantastic job calling us and looking after him... we'll be leaving for the hospital in a few minutes. Okay, that's fine. See you shortly.'

He ended the call and turned back to Mr Wilson. 'We need to get you to the hospital now, Mr Wilson. Make sure you're okay after the fall. Your blood pressure is low, so it needs to be monitored.'

'I was dizzy. Everything went fuzzy and black.' Fear returned to the old man's eyes.

'They'll look after you at the hospital.'

'We could go with him,' Alfie said.

Lee scowled and Alfie knew what he was thinking; if mum got home and they weren't in, they'd be in big trouble.

The old man's tight grip on Alfie's arm relaxed, but he didn't let go completely. 'Sings like an angel, this one.'

'You boys can stay while we finish here, but we can't take you with us. It's good to see you're so keen, though. We're always eager to encourage the next generation,' the paramedic said to Lee.

'We should be going home. Our mum will be getting worried,' Lee said.

The lady paramedic finished monitoring the old man and looked at them. 'Do you live nearby? It's awfully late to be walking around.'

'Just over there.' Lee pointed in the general direction of the flats.

'Best not keep your mum waiting then, boys,' she said.

They wheeled Mr Wilson out of the door. The ambulance was parked directly outside the house and the paramedics kept talking to him as they navigated the narrow path.

'Your daughter's only five minutes away. She should be here before we leave,' the male paramedic said.

Lee peered into the back of the ambulance, watching attentively as the paramedics made Mr Wilson comfortable. Alfie had to tap his brother's arm to get his attention. 'It was brilliant what you did,' Alfie said. 'You were so calm.'

'It felt good to help. Like what I was doing really mattered to someone for a change.' His voice cracked, and he coughed to hide it.

The big paramedic had been listening to their exchange. 'I think you'd be a natural for this line of work. St John's Ambulance run courses and gives training to youngsters. You should check into it.'

Lee shrugged, but his eyes were bright, as if the idea was taking hold.

A car pulled up behind the ambulance and a middle-aged woman jumped out.

She gave Mr Wilson a quick hug and spoke with the paramedics before agreeing to follow on in her car. While they shut the ambulance and prepared to leave, the daughter packed a bag for her dad and checked everything was secure before locking up.

The three of them stood and watched the ambulance drive away.

'Thank you both so much for all you've done. If this had happened when he was alone, he could have died.' She choked on the words.

'We're glad he's okay,' Lee said.

She looked at her car. 'I really need to get to the hospital, but I can give you a lift home on the way.'

'We'll get the bus. It isn't far.'

'It's past nine o'clock. Surely your parents will be worried sick.'

'Mum's at work. It's fine,' Lee said.

'Well, take this then…' she rooted around in her bag and handed them a twenty-pound note. 'You can get a cab home. Be safe. And thanks again.'

They waved as she left and then stared down at the money. 'If we walk, we can stop at the shop and get mum a massive box of chocolates with this,' Lee said.

They grinned at each other and started walking.

'So will you look up St Johns Ambulance?'

'Might as well, something to do.'

'You'd make a good carer. You always helped Grandad when he was alive.'

'It could be a good job, I suppose. I thought the ambulance was cool. Driving round with the siren on and everything would be outstanding, but the uniform sucks.'

Alfie laughed, but he could see Lee ending up just like the big, friendly paramedic they'd met. Better that than following dad to prison.

At the express supermarket, they bought chocolates and a chocolate orange bubble-bath set. Booty in hand, they started walking back to the estate, but stopped and hung back in the shadows. Two police cars were pulled up on the pavement, lights flashing. They were in the middle of arresting three people.

Alfie gulped, recognising a handcuffed Jonny being helped into the back of a police car. They stayed out of sight until the cars drove off.

'Good job you came along tonight, or I'd have been arrested too.'

'And Mr Wilson might have died if you didn't help him.'

Lee nodded, his expression grim. 'I guess I owe you one.'

'Don't worry about it.'

Lee was uncharacteristically thoughtful. 'At least we got mum presents this year.' He held up the bag and grinned before turning serious. 'We can't tell her about this, though. She'd go ballistic.'

'You saved someone's life.'

'So, I should never have dragged you along with me in the first place. I knew they were up to something. I'm sorry.'

Alfie let the words sit between them for a while. 'What about Jonny and the others?'

'I swear I won't hang out with them again.'

'But what if they tell the police about us?'

'We did nothing wrong, not really.'

Alfie considered everything that had happened in the space of a few hours, hoping the good outweighed the bad.

Lee ruffled his hair. 'You were brave tonight. You stood up to three bullies and did the right thing.'

'Cheers bruv.' Alfie punched him on the arm and dodged sideways when Lee tried to retaliate.

'Oh, you think you're hard now, little man?'

'Not as hard as my big brother,' he said.

'Yeah, well, Mum ain't gonna think the same if we roll in after her shift ends.'

They raced up the steps to the flats and this time Alfie managed to keep up.

CHRISTMAS WISH - PART TWO

Lynn slumped down on the bench and stared at her silent phone whilst sounds of merriment radiated from the pub. She should never have pushed Cassie into doing the pregnancy test tonight, not in the middle of their works do.

She downed a gulp of rum and cursed as she sloshed the dark liquid around her glass. Alcohol was the cause of so many of her problems, but it was the only way to get through the festive period. She wished it could be different, that she could enjoy Christmas like everyone else for a change.

Teeth chattering, she pulled the coat more tightly around herself. She longed for a cigarette to give her something to do, but she'd kicked the habit years ago. Now wasn't the time to indulge in any other bad lifestyle choices.

Lynn glanced down at her phone again. Still no word from Cassie. She sent a short, apologetic text and dropped the phone into her duffle coat pocket.

Please let the test be positive. Cassie deserved a baby; she'd be a brilliant mum.

She sighed and touched her own belly. What would it be like to be pregnant? She'd need a man first, and they were as elusive as Christmas elves.

The door to the pub opened, and she glanced up as light and sound spilled out into the darkness.

Harry stood haloed in the glow and broke into a grin when he saw her. Her heart skipped at that devastating, dimpled smile. He certainly lived up to their nickname for him - Hot Harry.

'I thought I'd find you out here.' He handed her a drink - ice and a slice of lime just the way she liked it.

'Thank you.'

'The karaoke's getting wild in there.'

'That's why I'm out here. I refuse to be dragged into it again.'

'I remember last time. You weren't that bad. In fact, it was a surprisingly good Gloria Gaynor performance if you ask me.'

She held her head in her hands – another drunken regret. 'The less said about that, the better.'

'At least you didn't murder the song, unlike the girls from accounts who are duetting right now. I had to get out before my eardrums started bleeding.'

She laughed; she'd forgotten how much she enjoyed Harry's company. Her department had nothing to do with the corporate side, so they only saw each other at social events. Just that, and the odd sighting of him around the office to sustain her crush.

He hovered by the bench, looking around the empty beer garden. Even the hardened smokers had escaped back inside. 'You look lonely out here. Where's Cassie?'

'She wasn't feeling well and went home. You could always join me.' She shifted over and patted the bench, glad it was too dark for him to see the blush creeping across her cheeks.

He sat next to her. At such close quarters, the pull of Harry's magnetism was even stronger, and the tantalising scent of his musky aftershave coiled around her.

'It's a bit nippy.' He was still in his work suit, top button undone, tie loosened and askew. He always looked smart, so the slightly dishevelled look did funny things to her insides.

She sipped her rum and coke to calm down. 'After a few of these, you don't notice the cold.'

He laughed and chinked glasses with her. 'Sounds like a plan.'

Their eyes met, and the air seemed to sizzle before they both turned away.

'So that bonus will be welcome this year,' he said.

'Yep, I've already mentally spent mine.'

'I've got a mate who works in the travel industry. I'm thinking of booking a break to escape all this festive bullshit.'

She gasped and stared at him. 'No way, that's exactly what I was thinking.'

'Do you hate the whole Christmas nonsense too?'

She thought for a moment as she sipped her drink. 'No, it's more a case of not having anyone special to spend the holidays with.' Her own honesty caught her off guard. Where had that come from? 'I usually go to my sister's and play the fun auntie, but...'

'You'd rather be yourself?'

Lynn nodded, shocked she was opening up to Harry of all people - talk about a turn off.

She'd fancied the pants off him since he started in the company eighteen months ago. They'd shared a brief drunken kiss under the mistletoe last Christmas, but nothing more.

'Let's take a look at some holiday deals, cheer ourselves up,' he suggested. Their legs brushed as he balanced his pint between his thighs and dug in his jacket pocket for his phone. 'I heard Derek saying the bonuses will be hitting our bank accounts on Monday, so there's no time to waste.'

They huddled together as he flicked through holiday websites on the screen. 'Are you a sun or snow worshipper?' He studied her as if trying to work her out.

She hoped he couldn't read her thoughts, which were far away from holidays, though scantily clad bodies did feature heavily in her imagination. She shivered as a gust of wind whooshed through the garden. 'Definitely a sun worshipper.'

'Good choice.'

He typed in their selection and scrolled down the list of last-minute holiday deals. Zanzibar, Cape Verde, Caribbean cruises, all sadly out of her price range, even with a tasty bonus.

'Look at that one.' She tapped the screen to open a Cyprus deal and oohed over the beautiful golden beaches and turquoise sea. 'Cocktails and swimming in the sea. That sounds like heaven right now.'

'You've just described my perfect holiday.'

She looked down the list of prices. 'What I can never understand is why it costs so much for a single traveller, all those single supplements…'

'You should call my mate tomorrow, see what he can do.'

'Great, I will.'

Once they'd finished drooling over sun-drenched holidays way beyond their salary, they swapped numbers.

'Maybe we should go in. You're shivering.' He put an arm around her and rubbed her arm. She was anything but cold with his body so close, but she didn't move, not wanting the moment to end.

Reluctantly, she downed the last of her drink and realised his pint was empty too. 'My turn to get the next round in.'

'It sounds safe to head back in,' Harry said.

The usual Christmas songs were blaring out and looking through the misty windows, Lynn could see the dancing was in full swing. She stood and adjusted her coat; glad she'd opted to wear her strappy cocktail dress even if it was impractical for a cold December night.

Harry opened the door for her. 'Come on, we'll sneak into the other bar.'

Giggling, they skirted around their drunken colleagues, who were too busy dancing to notice them.

'I guess the double bonus has livened everyone up,' Lynn said. Even the oldies were dancing tonight.

They sat in the quieter side with the locals and drank at the bar, chatting about Christmas and how it sucked being single at this time of year.

'I'm glad I found a kindred spirit.' Harry chinked glasses with her.

'Here they are!'

'Hiding in here's no good. Everyone must dance. Derek's orders.'

The girls from accounts dragged them to the cleared area by the disco lights that served as a dance floor. Lynn was pleasantly surprised when Harry took her hand and danced with her. She could feel the warmth of his skin on the small of her back; maybe dancing was a good idea after all.

'I'll protect you from those drunken wenches,' he whispered so close to her ear that she felt the briefest brush of his lips.

'My knight in shining armour,' she cooed remembering their works do in the summer at the Medieval Banquet – he'd cut a dashing figure in a knight's costume.

He had a wicked gleam in his eye as he spun her around the dance floor. 'Of course, I'm also protecting everyone else from another Gloria Gaynor moment.'

'Hey,' she slapped his chest, getting a cheeky feel of the taut pecs beneath the thin fabric of his shirt. 'You said I was good.'

'Oh, you are a karaoke queen, but you don't want to upstage the whole office. There could be a revolt.'

By 11 p.m. they were all danced out.

'Fancy getting out of here and finding somewhere to eat?' Harry asked.

'Let's get something properly greasy and disgusting.'

He laughed. 'In that case, there's a kebab shop near here. It has seating and everything.'

'Sounds posh.'

'I can't vouch for the quality of the food, though.'

'Doesn't matter.'

They left together. The girls in accounts nudged each other and pointed, but Lynn ignored them. She'd dreamt of spending time with Harry ever since last Christmas, and she wasn't about to let a bit of gossip ruin the opportunity for her this time.

Outside, the cold air slammed into her. 'See, we need a holiday to escape all this crappy English weather.' Her breath puffed out as if to emphasise her words.

It had rained, making the pavements slick. Her party heels slipped from under her. Harry caught her and they walked arm in arm along the Christmas lit streets. The London nightlife was still in full swing around them, but she barely noticed.

Walking sobered her, though it felt like a dream being with Harry. He was the most talked about singleton in the company. Everyone fancied him.

'Here we are,' Harry said dubiously as they reached the kebab shop and stared through the window at the indistinguishable slab of meat turning on the spit.

'Are you sure about this? We just passed a nice-looking curry house.'

'Nah, this is the only way to end a proper night out.' She headed for the door just as a hen party rolled out. Singing and giggling, they walked away munching on large portions of chips between them.

'See what I mean.' She winked at Harry, and he rewarded her with a killer smile.

The warmth and meaty aroma hit them in a wave. Lynn ordered first. 'A doner and chips, hold the naan and the chilli.' Harry ordered the same and paid despite her offering to pay her share.

'Five-minute wait on the chips,' the chef said, handing Harry his change.

From the half a dozen tables to choose from, they opted for the one nearest the back.

'Just going to use the facilities,' Harry said and disappeared through the only door that served as a customer toilet.

She dug out her phone and saw a message had arrived from Cassie an hour ago.

Guess what? You're going to be an Auntie!

A few seconds later, another message had followed.

Don't tell anyone!!!!

Lynn squealed in delight and called her straight away. 'Cassie, that's amazing.'

'Shh,' her friend whispered. 'We don't want anyone else to know, not until it's certain. And then, of course, Derek has his retirement plans for next year...'

'Cassie, don't panic, my lips are sealed.'

'Is the party over? It sounds very quiet.'

'I'm at a kebab shop... with Harry.'

'Hot Harry?'

'Yes.' She kept an eye out for his return, her thoughts already wondering where the night would lead.

'Don't do anything I wouldn't do.'

'Considering your condition, that's not saying much.'

Cassie laughed. It was so good to hear her happy.

'Harry's a good bloke. I've always thought there was chemistry between you two.'

'Let's hope I soon find out.' She sniggered down the phone just as the door to the toilet swung open. 'I better go.'

'Call me tomorrow with all the juicy details.'

Lynn smiled and put her phone away, still not able to believe Cassie's news.

Her stomach flipped as she met Harry's gaze. God, he was sexy, even in the garish lighting of a greasy kebab shop.

His warm brown eyes took everything in. 'Are you okay?'

'I was just checking Cassie got home.'

'Order's ready.' The chef called.

'I'll get it.' Harry brought over their plates of food.

They ate and laughed through the meal. It really wasn't great, but she barely tasted anything, anyway.

The hour was late, and the chef had given them several warning looks when they thanked him and stood to leave.

Outside, Harry turned to her. 'Can I walk you home?'

'It's a bit of a trek from here.'

'I'm fine with that. It's a nice night for it.'

She giggled to herself, imaging what 'it' could mean.

Harry offered his arm, and they strolled along. He didn't say it, but she had a feeling he didn't want the night to end either.

Lynn led them along the Thames. The wind had died down, but now the alcohol was wearing off the December chill seeped inside her coat.

'So, this friend of yours really does exist and he'll give me a discount on a holiday.'

'Of course. We'll call him together if you want.'

'Deal. I can't wait to take a break from this climate.'

He waved his arm to indicate the dark expanse of the Thames. 'Just picture the crystal-clear waters, the warm breeze, and watching the sun go down over the sea with a pina colada in hand.'

She rested her head on his shoulder and closed her eyes. 'It sounds magical.'

For a moment she was there on the shore with the sand warming her toes. But reality crashed like a cold wave over those dreams. What was the point in even considering a winter holiday? It would be no fun alone. She may as well go along to her sister's again. Four years on the trot without a plus one. That could be a record.

Harry took her hand and gave it a squeeze. 'Are you okay? Not regretting that kebab?'

She chuckled. 'I'm fine. I've had a much better evening than I was expecting, thanks to you.'

'Me too. Though it's a shame Derek forgot the mistletoe this year.'

Heat flooded her cheeks. 'Ah, the mistletoe incident. You remember that?' Egged on by Cassie, she'd practically jumped Harry that night. He hadn't pulled away and had seemed quite eager to continue, but she'd chickened out and gone home soon afterwards.

Harry stared down at her. 'To be honest, I've thought of little else for the last few hours.' His thumb stroked across her jaw as he gazed into her eyes. 'Mistletoe is my favourite Christmas tradition.'

The longing she'd tried to keep dormant for the last year burned through her with a vengeance. She stretched up on tiptoes and brushed his lips with hers. 'We'll just have to muddle through without it.'

***

The next morning, she woke up to find the bed empty beside her. She lay listening to the silence in the flat, the ticking clock mocking her.

How could she have been so stupid?

He'd used her and then snuck away without even saying goodbye. How could she ever face him again in the office? She'd have to hand in her notice, use the bonus to live on until she found another job.

Tears pricked her eyes. She'd never have picked Harry as the one-night stand kind of guy. Had she done something to scare him off? She wracked her brains, but as far as she could remember Harry had been a more than willing participant. They'd only fallen asleep as the sun started to rise.

As she resigned herself to a weekend of moping, she heard a whistled melody that sounded suspiciously like "I'm Dreaming of a White Christmas".

Harry appeared in the doorway. He was in his boxers, carrying two steaming cups of coffee and the bag of chocolate filled croissants from her bread bin. 'Morning.'

'Yes, morning.' She turned away, wiping frantically at the mascara that was no doubt smeared around her eyes and ran her fingers through her hair before giving her appearance up as a lost cause.

Harry put the cups on her bedside table and climbed inside the covers.

She ran her hand across his naked chest, feeling the taut muscles flexing at her touch. 'I thought you'd left without saying goodbye.'

'I would never do that to you. Besides, I've been thinking. We might get a better deal on a holiday if we pitch in together.'

'Go together, you mean?'

'Why not? We're both single and at a loose end over Christmas.'

They barely knew each other. Okay, they'd spent the night together, but that was a little different to a holiday abroad. She looked at him, really looked, seeing everything she'd ever wanted in the man laying almost naked in the bed beside her. Wasn't this what she'd fantasied about for the last year and a half?

And what was her alternative for the festive period? Squealing kids, board games, overcooked turkey and veg, getting drunk and passing out on her sister's sofa.

'You seriously want to go on holiday with me?'

'Yes, it'll be fun.'

She grinned. 'Okay. I'm up for it.'

He reached for his phone. 'Cyprus, here we come.'

The Icing on the Cake

Jess drew back the curtains and sighed. 'That damn car is still parked outside our house.'

Her husband groaned from under the covers. 'It's too early for this, love.'

Ignoring him, she scanned along the road for likely suspects. 'It's been a week. It must have been dumped. Surely, there's a way to check.'

'Maybe one of the neighbours has family or friends staying for Christmas.'

'Whatever the case, it's inconsiderate.'

'It's not as if it matters to us. The drive's big enough for both kids' cars when they arrive later.'

'If I had such a beautiful car, I'd keep it in a garage or something. I would never park it outside someone else's house.'

'Ah, I see what's going on here.' Duncan rose from the bed and looked at the convertible Ford Thunderbird over her shoulder. 'You're annoyed because it's your dream car.'

'I am not that petty.' She glared at him and tutted for good measure. 'I just can't abide inconsiderate people and the world seems full of them nowadays.'

He wrapped an arm around her shoulders. 'We've been married forty-two years, Jess. I think I know you by now.'

She felt the tension in her shoulders dissipate and let out a long breath. 'Okay, fine. I admit I may be a little jealous. But look at it. Who wouldn't want a mint condition Thunderbird like that? It must be worth at least thirty thousand pounds.' Not that she'd looked recently. She'd had more pressing concerns than motor cars. 'It's left out there to the elements and to thieves. It's near on criminal.'

Admittedly, their road did have excellent neighbourhood watch, so why had no one seen who parked it there?

Duncan's voice pulled her back to the present. 'I've never stopped you from getting one. We have the retirement money, and we could think about downsizing. If having a car like that would make you happy, I'd make the sacrifice without a second thought.'

She took a last, longing look at the blue Thunderbird before kissing her husband's cheek. 'You're very sweet, but no. This is our family home and I want the grandkids to enjoy it, just like Mindy and Stewart did growing up.'

'Whatever you say, love.'

'Now is not the time for frivolous purchases, not at our age.' She massaged her chest, her thoughts drifting. 'My Thelma and Louise days are well and truly over.'

She headed to the door, but stopped and turned back to Duncan. 'Get dressed. We have a lot to get done before everyone arrives.'

Hurrying downstairs, Jess smiled to herself; there was nothing like a family Christmas - everyone she loved gathered under one roof. Who needed a Thelma and Louise moment, anyway? She was perfectly happy as Jess Renley in her bog-standard Ford Focus.

The oven timer pinged. 'The turkey needs another basting.' Jess paused from laying the table and called out to Duncan.

'Don't worry, love, I'll sort it,' he answered from the kitchen.

'Thanks.'

She made the finishing touches and then stood back with her hands on her hips to admire the result. The formal dining room had been transformed and looked like it belonged on a feature spread in one of those supermarket own magazines. The extended table had a brand-new red tablecloth, which made the polished silver cutlery sparkle and snowflake design china gleam. Wine glasses with cream linen napkins were in position for the adults, while beakers and fun penguin paper napkins were set out for the children. Each of the eleven place settings had a golden Christmas cracker.

It would be a bit of a squeeze, but that was what family Christmases were all about. She remembered times in years gone by; the quiet ones, the raucous ones – every one of them filled with love.

Jess shut the door and hung the 'No Entry' sign on the handle. No one was permitted entry until tomorrow's Christmas lunch.

Next, she inspected the front room. Dozens of presents in shiny wrapping paper were under the tree. The tree lights twinkled, and the decorations glowed as they caught the light. Everything looked perfect ahead of the tiny terrors' arrival.

All the beds were made, and the travel cot was erected. This year they'd agreed to be super organised so they could enjoy every second of the big day.

She walked into the kitchen, smelling a mouth-watering mix of roast turkey and honey-glazed gammon. 'It smells like Christmas in here.'

Duncan pulled the bird out of the oven and then turned to grin at her. He was wearing her 'Top Chef' apron, which was funny as he never usually cooked more than beans on toast.

'Perfect timing. This should be just about done.' The meat thermometer soon confirmed his words.

The clock chimed three p.m. 'Only a couple of hours of peace left.' She took a breath; it was a long time since they'd had a house full over an extended period.

'Have a rest if you need to. I can finish here.'

'No, I'm fine.'

'In that case...' Duncan handed her a peeler.

Like a well-oiled machine, they prepped the vegetables and peeled two big pans of potatoes ready for parboiling in the morning.

Duncan hung up the apron and poured her a glass of baileys over ice.

'It's a bit early, isn't it?'

'Nonsense. Put your feet up, enjoy five minutes peace before the mob gets here.'

No sooner had she switched on the TV than the first carload arrived.

She opened the door, letting in a frigid blast of air. From the doorway, she could see the blue Thunderbird and realised how silly she'd been this morning. How could a piece of metal compare to having a happy, healthy family?

Two excited children were released from their car seats and charged across the gravel drive like greyhounds from the traps.

'Grandma!' They yelled.

She bent and hugged them both, almost knocked over with their enthusiasm.

'Careful of Grandma, kids.'

She untangled herself and stood stiffly, grinning at her daughter. 'It's fine, love.'

Mindy hugged her and then stood back to study her. 'How are you feeling?'

'I'm good. Stop fussing.'

'Let's get out of the cold.'

She shook her head at her daughter but didn't complain. It was nice to be loved and to have these precious moments with her family. Not so long ago, she'd thought she'd never see them again.

The kids ran riot through the house, cheering and looking for their cousins.

'This will be the best Christmas ever.' Teddy shouted as he passed by like a whirlwind.

'Sorry,' Mindy said, picking up their discarded coats and shoes and storing them in the cupboard under the stairs. 'They're really excited about the sleep over with their cousins.'

'I don't mind the noise of these little scamps.' Jess ruffled Kelsey's curls as the three-year-old tugged at her dress.

'Grandma, how will Father Christmas find us?'

'Oh, he knows everything, sweetheart,' she told her granddaughter.

Placated, Kelsey re-joined her older brother running circuits around the front room.

Jess sat down while Mindy and her husband unloaded their bags and put armloads of presents under the tree.

She put her feet up and nursed her drink. The ice had melted, watering down the Baileys flavour, but it was still her favourite tipple.

Her daughter eyed the glass disapprovingly. 'Should you be drinking that?'

'I'm fine to have one or two, Mindy. Please don't go on.'

Mindy pursed her lips but nodded. 'Sorry, Mum. I can't help worrying.'

Duncan sat on the edge of her armchair and put his arm around Jess's shoulders, giving her a squeeze. 'How about I put the kettle on?'

'That would be lovely.'

Headlights in the window signalled the arrival of Stewart's family, which set the youngsters bouncing up and down with excitement.

'Don't get up,' Mindy instructed as she rushed to greet the others.

Jess rested her head back against the armchair. 'I couldn't ask for a better Christmas.'

'And it's still only Christmas Eve,' Duncan said with a wink.

***

'Santa's been!'

Jess looked at the clock: 6 a.m. It seemed only yesterday her own kids were doing the same.

She took a moment to acclimatise to the early hour before slipping into her dressing gown and slippers.

Begrudgingly, six adults gathered in the front room and watched four over-excited children rip open their stocking presents, while the baby crawled around happily in the reams of discarded wrapping paper.

Jess soaked up every detail before enjoying a Bucks Fizz breakfast that Mindy and Stewart insisted on preparing for everyone. It was a messy affair, with kids covered in egg yolk and strawberry jam, but the house was filled with laughter, and that was all that mattered.

'Is it present time yet?' Kelsey asked, licking her sticky fingers.

'You've just opened about twenty from Father Christmas,' Mindy told her daughter as she helped clean off the worst of the food with wet wipes.

Their old family tradition was to wait until after lunch, a crafty way to bribe the youngsters into eating their dinner. Jess wasn't sure five children under the age of eight could be so easily bargained with today.

'Okay, you can all choose one present now,' Duncan said, surprising Jess; he was usually the strict one while she was the pushover.

The kids cheered as they raced from the kitchen to the Christmas tree. It still looked like a paper bomb had exploded in the front room. They waded through the mess and each child selected a present from under the tree with their name on, though Kelsey needed a little assistance from her big brother.

Once the children had opened the latest gift, Duncan stood in front of Jess and held out a small box tied with a festive ribbon. 'This is for you.'

Everyone stopped what they were doing to watch. Jess flushed. 'Oh, I can wait until later like everyone else.'

'Open it now,' he insisted.

'Go on, Mum,' Stewart urged.

She took the box. It was light, and she immediately pictured the type of jewellery it could contain.

'Merry Christmas, darling,' Duncan said as she undid the ribbon and lifted the cardboard lid.

Nestled in tissue paper was a key. She picked it up and frowned at the Thunderbird emblem on the keyring. 'What's this?'

'Your dream car, of course.'

'What?' She stroked the design on the keyring. 'Are you serious?'

'It's all yours.' The twinkle in his eye told her it wasn't a joke.

'You sly old dog.'

'Why is Grandad a dog?' Kelsey asked, making everyone laugh.

Jess blinked back tears and hugged her husband. 'You have a lot of explaining to do.'

'That can wait.' Stewart handed her a coat. 'Let's go check the old girl out. Or at least rev the engine.'

'You were all in on this?'

'Yes, I've been dying to get behind the wheel, but I couldn't risk spoiling the surprise,' Stewart said.

'For the record, I didn't agree to any of this. Dad should have discussed it with you first,' Mindy said.

Jess turned to her husband. 'It is a lot of money, Duncan.'

'It doesn't matter. I know you've always wanted one.'

'But how on earth did you pay for it?'

He looked sheepish. 'It was a scratch card win.'

'And you kept it a secret?'

'I had to, otherwise you'd never have let me buy you that car.'

'Thank you.' She hugged Duncan - her love, her strength, and then she shared hugs with her children.

'We're so lucky to still have you with us, Mum.' Mindy said, with tears in her eyes.

Surrounded by family, her heart felt good as new. 'I'm not going anywhere, darling.' Jess said, and she meant it.

They hugged again, and Jess was thankful for every extra moment she got to spend with her family.

'Why do they keep having snuggles?' Kelsey asked.

'I think because Grandma had a bad heart, but the doctors made it good again,' Teddy said matter of fact as he drove his Hot Wheels racing car in circles across the carpet.

'Oh, okay.' Kelsey carried on playing with her new doll.

'How much did you win, exactly?' Jess asked, dabbing at her eyes.

Duncan broke into a huge grin. 'Enough to buy that little beauty outside, a new set of golf clubs for myself, and I still had enough left over to give Mindy and Stewart a few thousand pounds each as well.'

'I can't believe you kept it a secret all this time.'

'After the year you've had, I was determined to give you a wonderful Christmas.'

Jess looked at her family; her grown-up children and their partners, their mucky kids running around like loonies, and her wonderful, caring husband. She thought she would explode with love.

'Having everyone here is the best gift I could ask for.' She looked down at the Thunderbird key ring. 'This is just the icing on the cake.'

'Expensive icing,' Mindy muttered.

Jess grinned across at Stewart and wiggled the key in the air. 'Come on then, let's go check her out.'

As she walked past the hallway mirror, Jess imagined herself wearing big sunglasses with her hair tied back in a scarf, just like Louise had done in the movie.

Maybe she wasn't past it after all.

NOT JUST FOR CHRISTMAS
(EXTENDED VERSION)

As Nick turned off the main road into the carpark, he glanced over his shoulder at his wife and daughter. 'Keep that blindfold on, Meg.'

Meg wriggled in the seat. 'But it's so itchy, Daddy.'

'Just a few more minutes, I promise.' He caught Nancy's gaze, and they grinned conspiratorially.

Pulling into a space, he waved to a staff member being dragged around the perimeter by an excitable cockapoo. It reminded him of his own early training disasters with Dexter and his hand tremored as he switched off the engine. Burying painful thoughts, he lifted Meg from the back seat, her blindfold still dutifully in place.

A gusty December breeze whipped at their coats as they huddled in the carpark. He stared at the large glass-fronted building and heard the distant bark of a dog coming from inside.

'Where are we? Can I look now, Daddy?'

He took a breath. 'Go ahead.'

Meg ripped the fabric free, surprise fading to confusion as she spied the big yellow sign with a dog's face on it.

'Are you sure, Nick?' Nancy whispered.

'We've filled in the forms and had all the checks done; it's time.'

His wife blinked away tears before crouching in front of their daughter. 'Honey, you know how Dexter went to heaven?'

Meg nodded, scuffing her toe in the gravel.

'We've decided it's time to share our lives with a new dog.'

Meg bit her lip, looking uncertainly between them. 'We're getting another dog today, like an early Christmas present?'

'Only if we find the right match. And we might have to wait a few days to take them home,' Nick cautioned, seeing the excitement grow in his daughter's wide eyes.

She squealed and grabbed their hands, dragging them towards the main building.

Meg paused outside the big reception door. 'Won't Dexter get sad watching us from heaven?'

'He knows we still love him. We just want to give a lonely dog a home,' Nancy answered.

'Dexter would like that,' Meg said with the unerring confidence of a six-year-old.

It was Nick's turn to swallow back emotion as he pictured the grey-muzzled Labrador passing away in his arms.

He held open the reception door and ushered his family through. Inside, pictures of happy families and their adopted dogs lined the walls. Every success story warmed his heart. Another dog saved.

The receptionist smiled at them. 'Can I help you?'

'We're the Shelton family. We have a 1 p.m. appointment,' Nick said.

'Take a seat and someone will be with you.'

They perched on one of the bright yellow couches. Nick tapped his foot, nerves fluttering in his belly. Nancy lay a hand on his knee and squeezed, offering him a reassuring smile.

He remembered meeting the gangly black pup, his faithful companion for twelve years. Dexter had given him a reason to carry on when the depression made him want to hide away. He'd even met Nancy because of the loveable rascal. She'd worked at the local pet shop and Dexter had taken an instant shine to her. Nick wasn't far behind on that score, visiting the pet shop far more times than was necessary, even with a growing puppy.

Without Dexter, Meg would not exist, and Nick's life could have taken a very different path.

Losing Dexter had been the hardest moment of his life. Nick's heart still broke whenever he thought of the tatty old teddy Dexter used to greet him with every time he came home from work. Could he knowingly consent to going through that trauma again?

He watched a couple leaving, led by a wagging spaniel wearing a shiny new collar. The couple were smiling, brought together by the special joy only a dog can bring.

Nick realised whatever dog they adopted wouldn't replace Dexter, but it would help fill the gaping void he'd left behind.

A lady emerged from the office and headed towards them. 'Are you the Shelton family?'

They nodded.

'Wonderful. Follow me. I think I have just the dog you're looking for.'

As they stood together, Nick glanced at his wife and nodded. He was ready.

Dexter had saved him at his lowest point. Now it was his turn to do the same.

***

'Buddy. No! Stop chewing the Christmas tree!'

Nick heard Nancy shout as he stepped inside the front door with his arms laden with shopping bags. Meg was giggling. He pictured her face screwed up with laughter as she egged on the naughty puppy.

He put down the bags and whistled. Seconds later, he was rewarded with the sound of nails skidding across the floorboards.

Buddy appeared as a blur of rust-coloured fur in the hallway and launched himself at Nick's legs. At nine months old, the gangly Vizsla still wasn't fully grown and had poor control over his limbs and chewing instincts. Having already been rejected by his two previous owners, he'd had a difficult start and lacked training and routine. But after a few timid days at home with them, Buddy was really starting to come out of his shell and bond with the family.

'Hey boy.' Nick crouched down and stroked Buddy's head and chest. After giving Nick a thorough licking, the puppy lay down at Nick's feet and enjoyed a tickle on the belly.

'Daddy!' Meg ran to greet him.

He was permitted a brief cuddle before his daughter ran screaming down the hall with a tug rope and Buddy trailing after her.

'Sometimes I think she's as crazy as the dog,' Nancy said, dodging out of their way.

'They make a perfect pair.' Nick slung his arm around Nancy and gave her a squeeze. 'How was your day?'

'Tiring.' She helped him into the kitchen with the bags. Between them, they restocked the cupboards in record time - much quicker than it had taken him to navigate the aisles of panic buyers. And it was still two days before the big day.

'I'm worried Buddy will never learn,' Nancy said after dinner as they retired to the front room with their cups of tea and collapsed on the sofa. 'Who gets a rescue dog just before Christmas, anyway?' Nancy groaned at the sight of the dustpan full of pine needles and chewed bark in the corner. 'And a real tree! We didn't think that part through.'

'He just needs to learn his boundaries,' Nick said. 'I'm not giving up on him.'

'I know, love. It's just hard to adjust to a puppy in the house.'

'We'll be able to take him out for walks soon, and I have time off work over Christmas so we can share the training.'

'Was it this hard with Dexter?'

Nick thought back to the early days with the tiny Labrador. 'Now I come to think of it, he was a nightmare, so clumsy and slow to learn. But look how he turned out.' They gazed at the large canvas photograph on the wall above the TV. Meg was a cheeky toddler with her arms around Dexter's neck. He'd been as gentle as a teddy bear with Meg and put up with no end of cuddles.

On the opposite sofa, Meg and Buddy were curled up asleep next to each other under a Christmas blanket.

'We just need to get through these teething problems,' Nick said. 'He'll be the perfect family pet, you'll see.'

'If the house survives,' Nancy said ominously.

***

'I hate him.' Meg wailed. Tears streamed down her face as she clutched the two halves of her toy rabbit.

'It's okay, sweetheart. Daddy can fix it.'

Leaving the supper preparations, Nick dried his hands on a tea towel and tossed it onto the kitchen counter. Then he picked up his daughter and carried her into the front room. Plonking her down on the sofa, he glanced around for the offender.

Buddy sat in his bed, cowering as he watched them. Nick's heart softened. How could anyone get angry with that adorable little face?

'Sweetheart, Buddy is still learning what he's allowed to play with. So just for now, I think you should keep your toys upstairs and out of his reach.'

Meg nodded but still cried with wracking sobs. 'Bunny's all broken.'

'I'll sew Bunny up and she'll be as good as new, I promise.' Nick cuddled his daughter, eventually feeling the sobs subside.

Sensing the worst was over, Buddy quietly crept towards them. He jumped onto the sofa and put a paw on Meg's arm. When she turned towards him, he licked away her tears. As soon as she started giggling, Buddy's tail began to wag.

Meg got down off the sofa and they played chase around the house.

'Best friends again.' Nick smiled to himself as he stood up. 'Now where's that sewing kit kept?'

He carried the decimated soft toy into the kitchen, tripping over half-chewed dog toys on the way. Cursing at the muddy footprints he'd yet to clean off the tiled floor, he grabbed a mop and checked the clock. He should have just enough time to clean it all up before Nancy got home from work. Christmas Eve was always a busy day at the office for her, and he didn't want Nancy to walk into a mess.

As he mopped the floor, he unearthed yesterday's newspaper torn to shreds under the table.

'So much for teaching Buddy what's his,' he said as he disposed of the soggy evidence in the recycling bin.

Next, he tackled the box of tangled cotton threads and chose a pale blue to match Meg's bunny. He sewed the head back on and reattached one of the ears before holding it out to inspect the result. It wasn't perfect, but hopefully Meg wouldn't mind.

He was just putting the vegetables on to boil when Nancy arrived home. Drying his hands again, he discarded the tea towel and went to meet her at the door.

'Honey.' He kissed her cheek. 'How was your day?'

'Busy. I've earned my week off today,' she said as she hung up her coat. 'Something smells good.'

'That's tomorrow's turkey. I haven't finished sorting the dinner out yet.'

'Have these little monsters been keeping you busy?' she asked as Meg and Buddy ran to greet her.

Meg pulled a scary face and growled at her mum before giving her a cuddle. Buddy joined in, running around them and barking happily in his own form of hello.

'Hello Bud.' Nancy patted his back. 'Try to keep the noise down. I'm getting a headache.'

'How about I run you a bath and you can relax before dinner?'

'That would be heaven.'

As Nick went upstairs to prepare a relaxing bubble bath, Meg dragged Nancy into the front room. He could hear his daughter chatting away. 'It's the last day of my advent calendar today. I saved it to do with you, Mummy. Father Christmas comes tonight. Will he bring a present for Buddy?'

He grinned to himself. Meg could be such a chatterbox and it was lovely to see her so excited about Christmas.

Nick tipped in lashings of lavender bubble bath and was just lighting Nancy's scented candles when he heard barking. Not Buddy's play barks or scared barks, but insistent something's wrong barks.

Heart in his throat, Nick rushed downstairs.

Nancy was just coming out of the front room with Meg trailing behind her.

'Stop barking, Buddy,' Nancy said, sounding irritated.

The puppy was standing at the kitchen threshold, barking at something. His stance was rigid, protective, almost.

Nick sniffed. Was that burning?

He raced past Buddy into the kitchen. The corner of the tea towel was resting on the hob. It was smouldering and smoking, and small flames were licking up the fabric.

Nick grabbed the tea towel by the other end and threw it in the sink. He turned both taps on full blast and watched the steamy smoke hiss away. He turned off the hob, annoyed at his own stupidity.

The others were gathered in the doorway, watching. 'Crisis averted,' he said.

Nick opened the back door and window to clear the smoke. Why hadn't the smoke alarm gone off? The green light was on. He mentally added checking the batteries onto his to do list.

'Thanks, Buddy.' Nick dropped to his knees and ruffled the puppy's fur. He sat quietly, nose up, and seemed to be quite proud of himself.

'He saved Christmas.' Meg declared. 'My dog is a hero.'

'Buddy just earned himself an extra slice of turkey, that's for sure,' Nancy said as she donned the oven gloves. 'And you've earned a rest from the kitchen, darling.' She told Nick.

'Oh god, the bath.' He raced up the stairs and got to the taps just in time.

When he returned, the turkey was resting under tinfoil and dinner was cooking.

The security light was on in the garden and through the patio doors he could see it had started to snow. A flurry of small flakes were falling and

Buddy and Meg were bouncing around, trying to catch them.

Nancy handed him a bottle of beer and then held her own bottle aloft. 'To Buddy.'

'And Dexter.' He smiled, remembering how much the Labrador had loved the snow.

Arm in arm, he stood with Nancy and watched their daughter play with Buddy in the garden.

It was good to have a dog around again. A home just wasn't right without one.

ONE GOOD DEED

'Your mum says you know how to use a till?'

'Yes, Uncle Barry.'

'Best just call me Barry while we're at work. Don't want people thinking this is nepotism, do we?'

Which, of course, it was, Sam thought. 'I worked part time in bars and cafes while I was at university.'

'Good. Then I'll just give you a quick tour of the shop floor before we open.'

Sam followed his uncle along the rows of used records and music books. There were sections for various musical instruments, and shelves of music related gifts and everyday items like guitar strings and tuners. Sam absorbed it all, though his attention was constantly drawn to the rows of guitars on the wall.

Uncle Barry saw the lingering look and grinned. 'When it's quiet, you can have a go on any instrument you like. And, of course, I expect you to demonstrate them to the customers when required. None of that thrash metal on the guitar, though. We don't want to scare them off.' Barry mimicked a head-banging rocker playing air guitar before he laughed and walked them over to the serving area.

Sam didn't comment; it was too close to the truth. No one wanted his music. Months of auditions and putting himself forward for session musician gigs had worn down his confidence.

After memorising the simple layout of the shop floor, Sam took a bit of time familiarising himself with the stock on the computer system.

'We open in five minutes.' Barry handed him an employee badge to pin on his t-shirt. 'And if you insist on having long hair, could you at least tie it back while you're at work?'

Sam grinned and did as he was asked; his long hair had been a source of gentle family teasing since he was fifteen years old. It reached halfway down his back now, and he had no plans to cut it.

Uncle Barry put him on the till for the first day. Time dragged as he waited for customers to come to him. To fend off boredom, he tidied the cupboards around the till and the cluttered countertop.

'How are you finding it?' His uncle asked after lunch.

'Nothing I can't handle.' Sam forced a smile, trying to remember that Barry was doing him a favour by giving him the job.

'It gets very busy in the run up to Christmas, so be prepared.'

That was still weeks away. Sam wasn't sure he could hack it that long, though he'd promised his mum he'd try.

At the end of the first day, he helped lock up.

'Why don't you play a bit of guitar before you head home? I've seen you eyeing up that Fender all day.'

'No, you're alright. I should get back.' Sam waved and left by the staff exit, refusing to give in to the unbearable itch to play guitar. He wasn't sure he ever wanted to pick one up again.

Sticking in earphones, he stuck his hands in his pockets and walked through the indoor shopping centre and out into the cold November evening. On the edge of the steps, tucked out of the way, an old man was sitting huddled in a long, padded coat. Sam frowned, certain he'd been there at the start of the day too. The stranger turned and looked at Sam as he passed. He was scruffy, but he didn't look like trouble, just sad and alone. Sam had helped at a homeless charity when he was at university and recognised the type. He nodded to the man and offered a smile, just so he knew he wasn't invisible.

***

The next day, Sam helped with a stock delivery and kept himself busy sorting and stacking the shelves during the quieter periods. Then he re-arranged the boxes of second-hand records on display to make the browsing experience more appealing.

Barry inspected his work. 'That looks good. Now let me show you these beauties.' Behind the counter, his uncle had a special collection of first edition records worth lots of money.

'You get the odd collector passing through,' Barry said as he locked the cabinet back up. 'Vinyl is big business if you know what to look for.'

Sam couldn't see the appeal of collecting old records when he could listen to any song he wanted on Spotify. But he could see it was his uncle's passion, so he nodded and feigned interest.

Mid-afternoon, Sam spotted the homeless man wandering the corridor outside the store. He wasn't causing any trouble and kept out of the way of the customers; Sam guessed he was just trying to keep warm and find something to do.

He also realised the man wasn't as old as he first assumed, maybe only in his fifties.

Barry noticed the direction of his gaze. 'That's Eddie. He hangs around all the time. Most of the shop owners don't have an issue with him, but I don't like the way he loiters outside my store, and I certainly don't let him play any of the instruments. The shopping centre manager won't do anything about him unless he becomes a nuisance, so we're stuck with him.' His uncle wandered into his office, grumbling to himself.

Sam disliked such short-sighted attitudes towards homeless people; most couldn't help being homeless. It wasn't a lifestyle choice.

A couple came in and wanted to discuss buying a second-hand keyboard for their daughter.

Barry nodded at Sam. 'My assistant can demonstrate a few for you and go through the type of features you may want to consider.'

Sam dutifully took the couple to the keyboard section where ten different models were on display.

'Has your daughter any experience with the instrument?' he asked, assessing the current stock.

'Only at school. We thought it would be a nice Christmas surprise. If she gets on with it, we'll think about booking her lessons in the new year,' the dad said, looking at Sam expectantly.

Sam gulped; selling was not his forte. He was more used to hiding behind his guitar and letting it do the talking for him. 'I read that playing an instrument is good for brain development. They've done studies on how it can even help kids achieve more academically.' Sam pulled the fact out of the dark recesses of his memory and the couple seemed impressed. Maybe he could talk his way through this.

Sam showed them several models while checking their reactions to the prices from the corner of his eye. The couple didn't look poor, but they clearly weren't super rich either. Why would they be looking at second-hand instruments in a department store if cost wasn't an issue?

'This is a good beginner keyboard.' He talked through its features and their price expectations.

'It looks nice,' the mum said. 'Could you give us a proper demonstration?'

Sam swallowed. 'Okay, though I'm a bit rusty.'

He picked an easy tune, Fur Elise, and then moved onto a more modern Adele track.

'You're good at that,' the dad commented.

Sam shrugged. 'I learnt to play a lot of instruments growing up.' He nodded towards his uncle, who was chatting to a customer at the till. 'Perks of having family in the business.'

'What's you preferred instrument then?'

'Guitar has always been my passion.' Up until six months ago, he added to himself.

The Uni band he'd played lead guitar in had begun to get a following and had played lots of local gigs. He'd thought they were set to make it big before the dream came crashing down. It was still a sore point. Just thinking about it was like lancing a boil on the most painful part of his anatomy. But he didn't think his uncle would be grateful for him sharing the dark side of music with prospective customers.

Sam stood and waved to the seat. 'Would either of you like to try it out?'

The couple looked at each other. 'No, that's okay. We'll take it.'

Sam found a box in the storage room and packed everything away before ringing up the purchase. The husband struggled under the awkward shape of the box while his wife carried a beginner keyboard book Barry had thrown in at half price.

'We may be back in the new year,' she said. 'Our son has taken an interest in the guitar.'

Sam's stomach constricted, remembering how amazing it had been to get his first guitar. Would he have bothered to learn if he'd known about the crushing defeat that lay ahead?

'We offer some great beginner packages for both electric and acoustic guitar, so keep us in mind.' His uncle stepped in when Sam missed the sales opportunity.

'We will, thanks very much.'

The couple left happy, and Uncle Barry patted Sam on the back. 'You're a natural at this. I'd say you've earned a coffee break.'

Sam gladly escaped the shop floor, needing to gather his thoughts.

***

Over the next two weeks, Sam's confidence in the job grew. He saw the homeless man, Eddie, most days, and they nodded to each other in passing. Sam wondered what his story was and why he always looked so longingly through the entrance to the shop. Sam had even caught him watching when he demonstrated the keyboards to customers.

'Do you play?' he asked Eddie one slow, wet afternoon as the older man shuffled past.

The man looked surprised and then thoughtful. 'Used to play... not much chance of it now, mind.' There was longing in his eyes and a hunger to indulge in a passion denied to him through whatever circumstances had seen him living rough. 'You're good. You've got music in your blood, kid.' He doffed his hat and walked away.

Sam pondered his words and glanced at the guitar area of the store. There were so many shiny instruments at his fingertips, and yet he was too scared to pick them up. Last year this would have been a dream part-time job between his studies. Now the only times he picked up a guitar were to check the tuning or to help a customer.

Where was that spark of desire, the love and passion for his music?

It was quiet on the shop floor, so he walked to the guitar section and allowed his gaze to roam over the instruments.

He picked up a black Stratocaster, similar to one in his own collection. A quick strum showed it was still perfectly tuned. Plugging it in, he slipped the strap over his shoulder and switched on the amp.

His fingers moved without conscious thought. He found himself playing the song he'd written just before the band split up; he'd never even had a chance to share it with them.

Music poured from his being, the guitar his voice, his soul. He ached as he played, realising how much he'd missed the simple pleasure of creating beautiful sounds.

'Nice to see you playing. Your mum's been worried about you.' His uncle commented when Sam returned to the serving area.

'I've been working through some stuff. She doesn't need to worry about me.'

'That's something you need to learn about parenting. You can't switch it off, no matter how old your kids get.' Barry had girls of his own, so Sam knew he was talking from experience. He hadn't seen his cousins in months. He'd let everything slide since the fleeting taste of success backfired.

'I have a proposition for you, Sam. How do you fancy being in charge on Thursday?'

'Um, okay I guess.'

'You've done really well these last few weeks and I've had no issues leaving you in charge over lunch breaks. This is the next step.'

'I can handle it.'

'Good. I've asked the Saturday girl, Janice, to come in and help.'

'Are you having a day off?'

Barry ran a hand through his thinning hair and grinned. 'No chance. There's a big record fair up town. I've managed to bag a table to exhibit my stuff after an acquaintance of mine had to pull out. It could drum up business for this place. Extra advertising is never a bad thing.'

'I'm happy to help.' Sam looked around the store. It would be a good test of his confidence.

'Cheers son, this means a lot.'

They locked up together, Sam taking charge as his uncle watched on. It suddenly dawned on him he'd be doing it alone in just two days' time.

The night before, Sam struggled to sleep and got to the shopping centre early. The head security guard greeted him. 'Barry told me you're in charge today. I'll pop by later. Make sure you're doing okay.'

'Thanks,' Sam said and waved as he took the steps two at a time up to the second floor.

He'd dressed for the manager's role today with a smart grey shirt and tie, though he still wore his skinny black jeans and cowboy boots. He'd tamed his long hair into a neat ponytail and pinned the 'Store Manager' badge on his left shirt pocket. Holding his shoulders straight, he marched to the staff entrance of the store.

A purple haired girl was waiting there. She wore a miniskirt and black tights with clumpy DMs. 'I'm Janice.' She stuck out her hand.

'Sam.'

While they switched on the lights and gave the store a quick once over, he found out Janice was two years older than him and lived at home with her parents and young son. Her family were helping her put herself through a home study law degree.

'You're very determined,' Sam said in awe of the petite go-getter.

'I am now that I know what I want. The hurdles in the way don't matter because I have an end goal.'

'Good for you.' Her attitude was inspiring, while he had a sociology degree and no idea what to do with it. What life goal could he boast about?

'Your uncle said you're a guitarist in a band.'

'I was,' Sam said, trying to let go of the lingering resentment. 'The band broke up when Uni finished, turned out we wanted different things.' His voice caught despite his best effort to act nonplussed.

'Then I get home from Uni and it's like the last three years of my life didn't happen. I'm back to square one. I'd pinned everything on them, and now my dreams are shattered.'

'You have to get yourself out there again, form a new band.'

'I suppose.'

An awkward moment passed, and they still had ten minutes before he was allowed to open.

'What music are you into?' Janice asked.

'You might say I have eclectic taste, but seventies rock is my era.'

'I love punk, the attitude really speaks to me.'

'A punk loving lawyer,' Sam said, studying her dark eyeliner and dyed purple hair.

'Why not?'

Sam laughed. 'Why not indeed?'

At 8.59 a.m. Sam took a deep breath and stood by the entrance. He pressed the button, and the shutters rolled open at 9am on the dot.

'Let's do this,' he said to Janice, rubbing his hands together.

It was a slow start, even though it was only a few weeks until Christmas. There weren't many customers about, mostly 'EMBs' - early morning browsers, as his uncle liked to call them.

Sam spotted the homeless man pass by on his usual circuit of the different department stores. He waved as Eddie looked in, his gaze as always lingering over the instruments.

He felt a pang of sympathy for Eddie, remembering how he'd felt playing guitar again after his self-inflicted break. His fingers were sore and tender from constant playing, but it was worth every second of pain to rediscover his love of music.

'Hi,' Sam called out, catching the older man's attention. 'Do you want to come in and have a play?'

Eddie looked down at his hands; they weren't the cleanest. He stared at them for a long time and then walked away without uttering a word.

Sam looked over at Janice. 'I thought it was a nice gesture.'

'Not if your uncle found out.'

Sam returned to the till, wishing he'd kept his mouth shut.

Ten minutes later, Eddie was back and stood by the entrance as if waiting for Sam to repeat the invitation. His hands and nails gleamed, and his hair was brushed back; he'd clearly tried to tidy his appearance.

Sam waved him forward. 'I'm Sam, the owner's nephew. Follow me.' He led Eddie to the keyboard section of the store and the instrument his uncle said he didn't mind customers having a play on.

'How can you tell who'll be the next Mozart if kids aren't given an opportunity to experiment?' Barry often said. It was because of Barry that Sam had discovered his musical gene, so he couldn't argue with the logic.

Eddie stripped off his coat and tucked it with his rucksack under the keyboard. He sat down and stretched his fingers before lightly stroking the keys. His eyes were bright, but he still hesitated. 'It's been a long time.' His voice sounded hoarse with emotion.

'What sort of music do you play?' Sam asked.

'Blues, classical, jazz, whatever's asked of me.'

'You're a session musician?'

He nodded. 'I played at a lot of clubs around London…' He touched the keyboard, his long pianist fingers dancing over the keys. The volume was low, but Sam didn't need to hear to know Eddie was a professional pianist.

Sam left him to reacquaint himself with the instrument. While he served customers, he kept an eye on Eddie. He looked less homeless in this setting; strangers passing by might even mistake him for an employee. It was so sad that people were judged on appearance and circumstances. Maybe if Uncle Barry heard Eddie play, he would change his view.

Sam cast the thought aside. His uncle wouldn't appreciate a lecture on the issues of society.

'You're welcome to turn up the volume. I always like to play my music loud.' Sam gave an indulgent smile and was rewarded with a small nod.

Eddie turned it up halfway and surprised Sam by playing pieces from the Nutcracker Suite.

It was jolly, festive music and a couple browsing the record section looked over, smiling. They lingered, flicking through each box of second-hand records and picking out half a dozen to buy.

'Nice to have some real music for a change. None of that awful radio nonsense where the DJ's love the sounds of their own voices,' the man said as he tucked his purchases away in his record bag.

'You can't beat live music,' his wife added. 'We met at a festival, you know.'

They discussed the music they loved. Sam slipped into the conversation his uncle's collection of original records behind the counter.

The couple browsed and bought a collector's edition live album reminiscent of their younger days. 'Hard to find beauties like this. Thanks very much.'

They left happy with their purchase while Eddie continued to play in the background, moving seamlessly from one song to the next.

Sam stopped to listen, surprised to hear 'Clair De Lune' played note perfect.

An older woman waiting to pay also looked transfixed by what she heard. 'What a beautiful piece,' she said.

Sam nodded, speechless.

'Beautiful playing,' she told Eddie as she passed him on her way out. 'I could listen to you play all day.'

Eddie looked humbled by the comment.

'That was amazing,' Sam said, handing Eddie a coffee.

Eddie nodded thanks as he took the drink. 'It's nice being noticed and not just ignored.' He sipped the hot drink, his eyes misting over.

'You can play as long as you want today,' Sam reassured him.

Eddie gave a grateful half-smile and played a jazz number next; fun and complex it was a world away from the classical pieces.

A harassed-looking mother with a whingy toddler in a pushchair came into the store and flagged Sam down. 'Hi, I need advice on the best headphones to buy for a teenager.'

The toddler whined and wiggled in the pushchair the whole time Sam tried to describe the different headphones available.

Eddie started playing 'Twinkle Twinkle Little Star' and the little boy stopped moaning and paid attention. The mum visibly relaxed. She shopped for other bits amongst the gifts and gadgets section while Eddie's repertoire of nursery rhymes kept her toddler entertained.

'That's a few more items off the Christmas list. I'm chuffed. I don't usually come in here.'

Sam rang up the purchases and smiled at her. 'We aim to please.'

Another man was queuing to pay and nodded over at Eddie. 'It's nice to have live music. Not many places do that nowadays.'

Eddie ran through a few Christmas numbers and seemed oblivious to the effect he was having on the customers.

'Shall I dash to the food court and buy us lunch? Beat the rush?' Janice asked when they hit a quiet spell.

'Sure.' Sam dug in his pocket and handed her a £10 note as he gave his order. 'Grab an extra sandwich and sausage roll for Eddie.'

Customers were happily browsing whilst they listened. Sam knew he wasn't imagining it; they were staying longer. If only Barry knew the power of live music, he thought, grinning to himself.

The woman who'd been in earlier when Eddie played "Clair De Lune", came back. 'I've been thinking about getting my husband a keyboard. He's always saying he wished he'd learnt. Seeing the gentleman play today made my mind up.'

'Do you want a beginner keyboard?'

'Yes, nothing too fancy.'

'This one has lights you can play along to, and you can adjust the speed to suit your skill level.' Sam had soon recommended the perfect keyboard and taken payment.

'My son will come with me and collect it tomorrow,' she said, storing the receipt in her purse.

Sam was just putting a big red sold sticker on the keyboard as Janice returned with their lunch.

'There's magic in the air today,' Sam said.

'I'm not sure your uncle would be so happy if he knew you were encouraging this.'

'But listen to him.' Eddie was playing Moonlight Sonata, filling the shop with beautiful music.

Janice nodded. 'He sure can play, but I would keep it to yourself if I were you,' Janice said as she went to the office to make another coffee.

Perplexed, Sam pondered the situation he'd put himself in. On his first day in charge, he'd made some great sales, but he'd also gone against his uncle's rules. What would Barry say if he found out?

***

The next morning, Barry looked up as Sam walked into the store. 'Profits are up. I don't know what you did but keep doing it!'

'People were getting into the Christmas spirit,' Sam said, wondering how much to tell. If Barry was in a good mood, maybe he wouldn't mind that Eddie had been in the store.

'I sold a keyboard yesterday, but the lady asked if she could collect it today with her son. It's all boxed and ready in the office.'

'Looks like I should leave you in charge more often.' Uncle Barry patted him on the back. 'I'll make a sales agent of you yet, Sammy boy.'

The woman arrived mid-morning with her son in tow. Barry got to the tills first and chatted with her while he checked her receipt.

'It's so nice to hear music played live in the shop, not all those pre-recorded tracks on a loop. It's nice to have that personal touch.'

'Music is important,' Barry agreed. 'That's why I love running this shop, giving people the opportunity to have music in their lives at half the cost.'

'It's commendable. And who knew he had such talent…'

'Morning,' Sam jumped in. 'You've come to collect the keyboard. I'll just grab it from the office.'

'I hope your husband enjoys it,' Sam said, waving her off.

'So that's your secret,' Barry said, moving to stand beside him.

Sam gulped.

'Playing to the customers while I'm paying you to work, eh? I don't mind, it's clearly been good for business.'

'I...'

'Don't let me stop you. Drum up as much business as you can.' He waved his arm to encompass the store and then wandered off to see if any browsing customers needed assistance.

Sam bit his lip, feeling bad that he hadn't taken the opportunity to mention Eddie.

'Janice is working this afternoon, getting in a few extra hours before the holidays,' Barry said, looking at the clock. 'I'll head out and do a bit of Christmas shopping while she's here. I'll only be a couple of hours.'

'We'll hold the fort.'

Later in the afternoon, Sam saw Eddie lingering outside the shop. He had a happier glow about him.

'My uncle's out. Did you fancy having a quick play on the keys?'

Eddie nodded, the eagerness unmistakable in his bright eyes.

Sam's heart warmed to bring a little joy to a man who'd obviously suffered.

After work, he spotted Eddie outside the shopping centre and stopped for a chat. They sat on the steps together and shared a chocolate bar.

'If you don't mind me asking, how did you fall out of the music business?'

'My world fell apart and I couldn't cope.' He didn't elaborate and Sam didn't push.

'Do you have a family?'

'A son.' Eddie pulled a worn picture from his pocket showing a teenage boy. 'It was taken over ten years ago. He'll be all grown up now.'

'If I had a dad, I'd like the chance to know him.'

'Even if that dad was me?'

Sam nodded without hesitation. 'You're not a bad person, you're just in a bad situation.'

'Thanks.' He sipped from the bottle of water Sam had given him.

'It's not too late to find your son.'

'No, I don't want him seeing what I've become.' Eddie's tone was harsh.

Sam didn't pursue the conversation any further. 'Do you have somewhere to go, to sleep and get a warm meal?' He asked tentatively.

'There's a shelter I go to, not far from here.'

'That's good.' Sam stood and stretched. 'My bus is due soon. See you around Eddie.'

'Bye Sam.'

Eddie's situation filled Sam's thoughts as he waited for the bus at the end of the high street. He wished there was something more he could do.

***

'You've done it again,' Barry said as Sam prepared to put out more stock.

His uncle was checking over the accounts and sales. 'All that time prating about at Uni, and it turns out you're a closet sales whiz.'

'I wouldn't go that far.'

'I'm happy I brought you on board. I know you only planned to work here for a few months, but I think there's a future for you in this business.'

'Thanks,' Sam said, though in his heart he knew it wasn't what he wanted. The music was inside him. Selling other people's work would never fulfil him.

Sam cleared his throat. 'I was thinking. Live music has really been a success with the customers. Why don't you make it a regular thing? Allow people to perform here. They get free publicity, and you get to entertain your customers while they shop.'

Barry rubbed his chin and looked thoughtful. 'It could work. I'll give it some consideration.'

The following week, Sam asked Eddie to play again while his uncle was away. 'I got you this.' He handed Eddie a Santa hat.

Eddie took it with a smile and plonked it on his head. He was already wearing a red Christmas jumper with snowflakes on it, which he explained was given to him by a volunteer at the shelter. It was a little threadbare, but he looked the part to play some festive tunes.

'I was thinking of telling my uncle about you.'

Eddie shrugged. 'Your funeral.'

'Probably.'

Eddie played while Sam served customers alongside Janice. It was busy enough to keep them both working non-stop, but when it quietened down, Janice pointed over to the guitars.

'Why don't you join him for a quick duet? I can cover here.'

'I suppose.' Sam grabbed an acoustic guitar and walked over to Eddie. 'Fancy playing something together.'

'Sure.' Eddie looked relaxed and completely at home behind the keyboard. 'You know "Happy Christmas" by John Lennon?'

Sam nodded and strummed the intro. There weren't many people paying attention, so he sang. Eddie nodded and smiled encouragement. Sam lost himself in the performance. He hadn't realised how much he missed playing with other musicians until that moment.

As the song ended, Eddie programmed in a new sound on the keyboard. 'How about this one?' He played the opening and Sam had to grin at the iconic start of "Wonderful Christmastime" by Paul McCartney.

Customers gathered around and clapped at the end. Grinning, Sam hi-fived Eddie.

He glanced over to check that Janice was coping okay at the tills and saw Barry standing next to her.

Janice winced and mouthed sorry.

His uncle's face was red, as though he was biting down his anger.

'Thanks for listening. Enjoy the rest of your Christmas shopping.' Sam hung up the guitar and headed to the office behind the till where his uncle was waiting for him.

'So, this is your little secret? Letting the homeless in off the street to play on my equipment.'

'The customers were enjoying it. And you've seen the results. They stay longer and fill their baskets. Eddie has been good for business.'

'I don't care about that. I care you lied to me, that you went behind my back.'

'I didn't lie…'

'But you did go against my wishes. I gave you a position of responsibility and you abused it. God knows what your mother will say to this.'

'You're firing me?'

'I don't know, Sam.' Barry slumped into his chair. 'I just don't know if I can trust you anymore.'

A knock at the door broke the silence. 'Can I get some help out here? It's manic,' Janice called through.

Barry nodded for Sam to go and help. 'We'll discuss it later.'

Sam returned to the shop floor. The queue of people waiting to pay was building, but looking beyond the customers, Eddie was nowhere to be seen.

***

After work and another earful from his uncle, Sam found himself dragged down the pub by Janice.

'Barry said I should take a couple of days off. Come back in on Tuesday,' he said, moping into his pint. 'I've never seen him like that before. He's always been the happy-go-lucky uncle.'

'He was happy until he realised who you were playing with. He just needs a little time to cool off.' Janice nudged his arm. 'And if we've both got tomorrow off, you can buy me a drink.'

Over the weekend, Sam focused on his music. Playing with Eddie had stoked the flame inside him, and he started creating songs again. By the time Tuesday rolled around, Sam was raring to get back onto the music scene. But first he had to keep his promise and work at the store until his uncle could fill the vacancy.

Sam dragged himself to work after sleeping through the alarm. He missed his bus and rolled into town late. There was no sign of Eddie outside the shopping centre. Inside, the place was heaving with shoppers, so he had no chance to look for Eddie through the busy walkways.

Taking a deep breath, he walked into the store, preparing to face Barry.

'There you are. Come on, you're needed,' Barry said, with no hint of lingering anger or disapproval.

Sam fitted straight back into the role and helped at the till. The EMB's had turned into paying customers so they were busy from the start. In a brief reprise, Barry pulled a rolled-up sheet of paper out from under the tills.

'It's something I've been working on. What do you think?'

It was a mock up poster showing a stage fully kitted out with a drum kit, guitars, bass, and keyboard, but no performers. The words above it stated:

Live music coming soon.
Sign up to audition now.

'You liked my idea!' Sam grinned.

'But I'll need help to get everything set in motion.'

'I'm your man.'

'Are you sure? I know you want to be a full-time musician.'

'Who says I can't do both?'

'Good, because your first audition has just arrived.'

Sam turned and was stunned to see Eddie walking through the door. He looked different. His worn parka had been replaced with a fur-lined trench coat that looked suspiciously like Barry's old coat. Sam turned to his uncle. 'What's going on?'

'I found Eddie the evening after the two of you performed in my shop. I'd had time to think and felt bad for the way I'd treated you both. We had a long chat over a fish and chip supper. Turns out we have a lot in common, not least a love of music.'

The two men nodded to each other. 'Seeing as the customers enjoyed the music, I've asked Eddie to perform here over the festive period. A job of sorts, to help him get back on his feet.'

Barry patted Sam on the back. 'I want you to know there'll always be a job here for you, too. You could even oversee this performing venture. Who knows where it'll lead?'

'I'll do you proud, Uncle.'

Sam walked over to Eddie and shook his hand. 'I hear you've got the Christmas gig here. Bit of a come down from the London clubs.'

Eddie smiled as he stripped off his coat to reveal a different Christmas jumper beneath – this one green with jumping red reindeers. The Santa hat appeared from his trouser pocket. 'Nothing wrong in bringing some Christmas cheer to the world.'

Sam looked around the store, shoppers bustling, everyone rushing to prepare for the holidays. Music could help them all take a moment to step back and enjoy what this time of year was supposed to be about.

'I'm so glad my uncle gave you a job,' Sam said, seeing the employee badge on Eddie's jumper.

'He's given me something few others would - a chance to start over. I'm hoping to get my life back on track and then I can contact my son. It's all thanks to you.'

Sam nodded, too choked to speak. One simple act of kindness had changed a man's life.

'Happy Christmas, Sam.' Eddie doffed his Santa hat and then sat down at the keyboard to play.

Dear Reader

I hope you've enjoyed this collection of short stories. Please consider leaving a review and telling your friends about my books. Every review can help new readers discover my work and it's a wonderful way to support an author.

If you want to get in touch, you can use the contact form on my website. You can also keep up to date with new publications by joining my mailing list (links on my website) or following my author page on Amazon.

Also by the Author

Short Story Collections

Fantasy Short Stories
Love, Loss and Life In Between
A Christmas Wish

Fantasy Books

Silent Sea Chronicles Trilogy:
The Lost Sentinel - Book 1
The Sentinel's Reign - Book 2
The Sentinel's Alliance - Book 3
(Also available as Silent Sea Chronicles Box set)

Standalone epic fantasy:
Visions of Zarua

Starlight Prophecy
(COMING SOON)

Romance

The Mermaid Hotel Romance Series
(COMING SOON)

Acknowledgements

Thank you to my writing friends at Ashford Library Creative Writing Group. Our monthly writing and critiquing sessions have kept me writing and are always fun.

Special thanks to those who've helped with my crazy plan to get 'A Christmas Wish' ready in time for Christmas 2022.

About the Author

Suzanne lives in Middlesex, England with her husband, two children and a crazy spaniel. Her writing journey began at the age of twelve when she completed her first novel. She discovered the fantasy genre in her late teens and has never looked back. Giving up work to raise a family gave Suzanne the impetus to take her attempts at novel writing beyond the first draft, and she is lucky enough to have a husband who supports her dream - even if he does occasionally hint that she might think about getting a proper job one day.

An author of four fantasy novels including Silent Sea Chronicles trilogy and a Czech translation of her debut, Visions of Zarua, Suzanne hopes the dreaded 'W' word will never rear its ugly head again!

Suzanne collects books, is interested in history and enjoys wandering around castles and old ruins whilst being immersed in the past. Most of all she loves to escape with a great film, binge watch TV shows, or soak in a bubble bath with an ice cream and a book.

Find Suzanne on her website for information about new releases and follow the link to join her mailing list. www.suzannerogersonfantasyauthor.com
Twitter @rogersonsm

Instagram @suzannemrogerson
Facebook @suzannerogersonfantasyauthor